Keres
Fated Dragon Daddies
Book 6

Pepper North

Pepper North
With a Wink Publishing, LLC

Text copyright© 2025 Pepper North®
All Rights Reserved

Pepper North® is a registered trademark.
All rights reserved.

NO AI TRAINING: Without in any way limiting the author's [and publisher's] exclusive rights under copyright, any use of this publication to "train" generative artificial intelligence (AI) technologies to generate text is expressly prohibited. The author reserves all rights to license uses of this work for generative AI training and development of machine learning language models.

Prologue

Nestled in the center of a ring of imposing mountains, the village of Wyvern has existed for hundreds of years. Its quaint town center wraps around a square featuring a commanding dragon statue elevated on a block-wide platform for all to admire. The words chiseled into the risers of the stone steps are a mystery to most. Almost all the ninety-plus commemorative etchings feature the last names of the founding families of the town without explanation. During the prosperity of technological tools, most forgot the old ways.

One female descendant of each founding family has traditionally served as the keeper of knowledge. Passing a huge tome from generation to generation, that woman ensures the pact the original settlers made with the first inhabitants of this land can't be forgotten. The agreement between the huge, lethal creatures living in the mountaintops and the struggling, besieged humans sealed the duties for both sides. Promising protection for the people and fated mates for the dragons, this pact has evaporated from the minds of most of the citizens of Wyvern. But the dragons have not forgotten.

When all things powered by technology suddenly ceased to

function, the worst features of humanity erupted as people struggled to survive. Once again, the strength and power of the massive beasts who have guarded the city is needed. Revealing themselves to the current-day citizens, the dragon horde fulfills their promise.

As descendants of those original families are found, mate bonds are forged between dragons and humans. The old ways are essential to the survival of all, and the ancient pact will soar in importance once again. For there are dragons, and they hunt for more than prey.

Five dragons of the horde have recently discovered their mates in the growing population of Wyvern. Others still search, hoping that each day brings their mate back to their ancestors' home. The stakes are dire for the shifters. Mates create a balance between their human and dragon identities. One teeters on the brink of madness without the companionship of a mate.

Chapter 1

Flames heated the sky in front of Keres. He snapped back into his own mind mid-plummet. Ahead of him, a young amethyst dragon frantically flapped his wings in a desperate attempt to stay in front of Keres. A few more minutes and the last of the smaller dragon's energy would run out. Keres could end him with one snap of his powerful jaw.

Keres shook off the blood lust that sizzled through his veins. Seizing control, Keres diverted from his target and flew in the opposite direction without another look at his prey. The black dragon wanted to end the usurper for daring to appear on the horizon. Even though Keres was miles from his territory, he'd reacted as if the other dragon had trespassed. His lack of control both angered and frightened him.

And I had no idea what was happening.

The animal side of him had taken complete control, pushing Keres's logic and reasoning out of his skull. A roar burst from his throat as a final warning to his victim, who had disappeared from view as his dragon refused to back down completely. His jumbled thoughts continued to untangle until Keres could think rationally.

Still pissed off, he headed toward his mountain. Keres could isolate himself there until he was totally back in control. A movement to his left made him wheel around to face the incoming threat. Claws ready to attack, Keres readied his fire.

Keres! Stand down. Two mates are here. Drake's voice echoed in his head.

The alert didn't process. Battle lust raged inside Keres. How dare the dragons approach his territory? He would teach them a lesson they'd never forget.

Rising into the sky, he loomed over the bronze, blue, and gold dragons. While he recognized them as those of his horde, Keres didn't think past them trespassing on his land. He screeched with anger, not to warn the invaders, but to make sure his voice was the last thing they remembered.

Keres! Please don't hurt my Daddies!

The quiet voice sounded both scared and brave. That made him hesitate and allowed Keres a moment to think. He couldn't attack horde members. They were the only ones he trusted. Shame filled his heart.

Skye. Tell your Daddies to leave my mountain!

Keres? You're over Ardon's lair. We're going to visit for a tea party with Aurora. Come join us. You must be hangry.

Her sweet logic rocked him out of the blood rage filling his thoughts. He looked around and discovered Skye was correct. He wasn't on his land.

Wheeling, Keres headed for his lair. Drake, Oldrik, and Ardon sent him messages he didn't bother to hear. It would be the same old *Keres, you have a problem*, panicked message they'd sent repeatedly the last few weeks.

Keres, I'm worried about you. Skye's voice registered on him. He could feel the concern in her thought.

Shaking away the last of his anger, Keres knew he had to face the truth. He was losing it. This was not the first time he'd

4

snapped out of a fit of rage and violence. Without his own mate's gentle influence, the dragon inside him chose violence over sanity. Keres couldn't ignore the risks anymore. He'd almost injured Skye and Aurora.

His top-level staff had refused to follow his directions to close his estate. They'd finally agreed to operate without him for one year. After that time period, if he hadn't returned, they'd meet with all those who worked on his territory and made his land their home to undertake the process of readying his estate. The horde would need to invite another dragon to take his place. Keres didn't allow himself to dwell on this. *Mine.*

Even through his frustration, Keres appreciated they were loyal and not willing to give up on him. Stalking out of the estate, he sent a message to the only dragon shifter who could possibly help him.

Oldrik. I need to meet with you alone.

Ardon and I can leave Skye when she naps. Want to meet on the field at the west side of town?

No Ardon. I need you to come alone, Oldrik. I promise you are safe.

I don't need Ardon to protect me, Keres. Oldrik's voice resounded with anger.

Of course you don't. I'll rephrase that to tell you I'll scan for traps. I meant no offense.

Good. This afternoon at three?

Arriving at the meeting location early, Keres scouted from above before landing. Paranoia apparently went hand in hand with flashes of rage. Keres forced himself to focus and release the aggression that easily built inside him.

Keres shifted and waited for Oldrik to arrive. When the

sun glinted off bronze wings, he relaxed slightly. Oldrik had come. Battling the black thoughts that lurked in the corners of his mind, Keres realized he'd almost waited too long to have this conversation.

"Oldrik. Thank you for meeting me."

"I don't enjoy discussing anything without my mate and Ardon. You said this was urgent," the dragon shifter stated bluntly.

"Tell me where your sister is." Keres got straight to the point.

"Why?" Oldrik asked.

"You know why. It's the end for me. I'll replace myself for the horde."

"Your mate might be on the next transport," Oldrik pointed out.

"The numbers of those arriving have dwindled to a handful every month. The list of missing Wyverns is blank, except for a few older people. No more mates are arriving now, Oldrik. I have to face the truth. There isn't a mate for me in this generation. I can't last for another one. It's over for me. Tell me where she is."

"I can't do that for her safety, Keres."

"I will swear an oath to you. Over all these years, I've proven to you my word, once given, is solid. That hasn't changed. I will treat her well."

"I'm not sure exactly where she is."

"Tell me everything you can. I'll find her," Keres assured him. "I need a hint of where to start."

Keres studied Oldrik's expression as the bronze dragon considered his options. Rare female dragons battled for survival as shifters doomed to madness sought them as a last option. He couldn't imagine a life that didn't involve flight and freedom—all those things a dragon craved. For eons, females existed only to give life to new dragons. The procreation process couldn't be easy for them, taken by a dragon barely holding on to sanity without a mate bond to make it pleasurable.

Keres met Oldrik's gaze. "I will plead my case with your sister and hope she will help. I will accept no as an answer. Death will come to me either way. I will not drag an innocent into the torture that besieges me."

"I have your word on that?" Oldrik's focus was laser sharp.

"You have my word."

"The last I heard, she was in a small hilltop in Montana. I do not know the town's name or have an address. Rimi mentioned the construction of a new sports arena that might force her to move."

"Thank you, Oldrik."

"Bring her back, Keres. She deserves to live in the light."

Keres met his gaze and nodded. There wouldn't be a good end for him, but perhaps something positive could come out of this. The horde would protect his offspring and Oldrik's sister.

Every day Keres battled the urge to return to his territory. What could the other dragons in his horde do? He could take them. The violence that echoed within his brain made him fearless.

A thin sliver of reality remained inside him. These were the members of his horde. Together they had fought shoulder to shoulder, protecting each other as well as the citizens of Wyvern. Deep in his brain, the need to keep them safe overruled the growing blackness of his soul. It was better for him to keep searching—hundreds of miles from his allies and their mates.

He forced himself to stay away. Ranging farther and

farther, Keres scoured the area below for the only being who could help him regain himself. Rimi.

One month into his search, Keres circled over a medium-sized city. Montana had proven tough to scout. It was a big state with large empty spaces. Every time Keres thought he might have found a mountain with a view of a partially constructed arena, his investigations had resulted in eliminating it. Hell, by this time, he was searching for any type of construction.

The current city had a university with the footings of a new football stadium abandoned in a field. The community had repurposed the materials and supplies had gone to serve the residents. Going to college and defeating rival football teams were a thing of the past now.

After landing on a mountain crest, he watched the people moving below. On closer inspection, it was obvious this wasn't a functioning community. Bands of armed men roamed through the street. At times, an individual would dart out into the open at full speed and retrace their steps with their arms full. In random places, including in the middle of the street, bodies lay still. From the stench that reached him, they'd lain there for a long time.

This was the opposite of Wyvern. Some had grabbed power and forced their authority on the city dwellers. The supplies in the store had to be nearly depleted by now. He couldn't spot a garden or livestock area. The next winter would eliminate the townsfolk. These people were already dead. They simply hadn't realized it yet. Keres didn't feel sorry for them. They'd done it to themselves.

Too bad the forefathers of this settlement had not created an agreement with dragon protectors. Keres turned his attention to the mountains with a view of the stadium. Two stood near the construction site. Neither had an opening he could see.

Keres chose one randomly and spiraled around it from base to tip. Nothing. Not even a small crevasse that someone might catch glimpses of the construction site through. His investigation of the second yielded the same results.

Time to move on. Wait. What is that?

Battling the hope that kindled inside him, he headed for a mountain some distance from the two overlooking the arena. Was that an opening? It was on the side but would still provide a view of the area.

A much better location.

A dragon concerned about his or her safety would wisely choose that mountain over the others. Keres stifled his excitement. This could be another dead end.

Were those claw marks on the ledge? *Yes.*

Keres considered his options. Enter and see who was inside or observe from a distance. His claws gripped the rocky edge of the opening before he realized he'd decided. He strode confidently inside.

I am Keres, horde member of Oldrik.

Silence answered his announcement. Could the resident dragon have abandoned the cave before he arrived? Fury sparked in his gut. If he was too late.... Fighting back his desperation, Keres sent out a louder message. If Oldrik's sister was inside, she had to hear him.

Rimi. I mean you no harm. I promised Oldrik I would simply talk to you.

A scent wavered in the air. Keres lifted his snout to inhale deeply. What was that deliciousness wafting toward him? Something he'd never experienced before. He walked further into the cave. Keres threw himself backward when a movement whispered from his left.

Pissed, yet impressed at the same time, Keres considered the massive, sharpened blade that now swung harmlessly back and forth across the entrance. Had he not moved to the side instinctively, his head would now be rolling around on the stony floor.

Not nice, Rimi. You need to work on how you greet your guests.

Guest! Try invader! Turn around now, dragon. That was the easy one to avoid.

He controlled his reaction to her response. He'd found her! *What is that smell, Rimi? It's delectable.*

She didn't answer him.

Cautiously, he continued into the cave. The entrance split. On the right, spiderwebs decorated the ceiling, and the ground looked undisturbed. Tracks led down the path to the left. Keres could see the scrape of scales along the walls. That was logically the frequently traveled way, but that scent came from the unused one.

Trusting his nose, Keres chose the unused trail. Whatever that appealing aroma was, he needed to find it. Three steps in, a rumble to his left told him the other tunnel had just collapsed. A chuckle escaped his lips. He couldn't wait to meet the kickass dragon who'd tried to eliminate him.

Too obvious, Rimi.

A fifty-fifty choice. The odds won't be so good for you soon. Better go back and save your pretty scales.

You think I'm pretty? Aw. Thank you, Rimi.

Why are you here, Keres?

I'm losing my mind. I've been without a mate for too long.

Such a sad story. It doesn't answer my question. Why are you here?

To save my horde the trouble of killing me. Keres was almost to the end of the passage. She would have to make another move soon.

So, you came here for me to kill you?

No. I wouldn't put that burden on anyone.
You came here to die?

Keres didn't answer. An inner chamber glowed through the doorway ahead. What safeguards waited there? He considered the slight downward slope of the passage. Gravity might help him here.

After scanning the walls, Keres picked out a large round stone. He coaxed it out from its resting spot with his paw, working as silently as possible. When it slid free, he gently kicked it, rolling the roughly two-hundred-pound rock through the opening like a goal-earning soccer ball.

Flames rolled toward him. Keres ducked his head to protect his eyes from the blast and enjoyed the fiery bath. When it ended, he forced away his disappointment.

Still here, Rimi. I'm a black dragon. Remember my pretty scales? It would take at least ten times that amount of firepower to end me.

A second round of fire blazed through the opening. It lasted four times longer. Towards the end, the intensity fizzled out to a gentle warmth. She was out of energy.

Chapter 2

Keres strolled into the large chamber. He scanned the area. Where could she have gone? That alluring scent still wrapped around him. She had to be here somewhere.

Rimi. Where are you hiding? I know you're here.

Silence filled the cavern. A flicker of light caught his attention. Keres glanced to the left. Just like a malfunctioning lamp, some of her scales sparkled before morphing back to blend into cave wall. Inside, his dragon did a happy dance. Look how special his mate was. Just her scent had pushed the darkness from his mind. He craved her with every fiber of his being.

Rimi, you're out of energy. I know where you are. I won't hurt you.

The mossy, craggy cave wall disappeared. Keres stared at the vision in front of him. A crystal dragon sparkled in the glow of the torches illuminating the cavern. She struggled to raise her head to meet his gaze. Her eyes blazed with hatred.

Go away! I will never submit to you.

Her dragon shimmered as she shifted into her human form. Rimi grabbed a large butcher knife and pressed the tip to her chest.

Wait! He shifted faster than he'd ever changed in his thousand plus years. Speeding toward her as soon as his feet landed on the ground, Keres listened to that voice inside him urging him to do anything to save her.

He could smell the coppery essence of her blood when his hand wrapped around hers. Rimi screamed as pain lanced through Keres. He ignored the burning sensation on his hand. It wasn't important. Had he stopped her in time?

Controlling the knife she still held, Keres jerked both of their hands to the side roughly, and the blade clattered to the ground. He wrapped one arm around Rimi, securing her tightly against him as he ripped the shirt from her body to check the wound. Blood oozed from a cut between her breasts.

Oozed. Keres fixated on the word. If the blade had successfully reached her heart, the flow would be unstoppable. He pressed his palm to her chest and concentrated. His hand glowed red for several seconds. His prey burst into action, flailing her arms and legs to escape.

"Ouch!" Keres glared at the petite shifter struggling in his arms. "You kicked me."

"Get your hand off my boobs!"

"I'm sealing your wound, Rimi."

"I don't care if you're raising me from the dead. Get off me!" She grabbed his shoulders and pushed.

Keres didn't budge. He did lift his hand from her skin, enjoying the view of her pink tipped nipples as he checked out his handiwork. The wound no longer bled. "I think you'll live."

"Get off me, I said," Rimi said, shoving him away.

This time, Keres allowed her to scramble away from him. After moving a scant distance away from him, she paused to sweep her long, white hair over her exposed breasts as she glared at him. She was glorious. Her fierce bravery thrilled him.

Rimi swayed as she stood, and Keres reached an arm out to steady her.

"You need something to eat," Keres admonished.

"No kidding. I can't go out there. The world is madder than ever. A guy shot at me with an Uzi the last time I went out. This stupid town had already slaughtered all the livestock. And now you're here to force me to defend myself and zap the last of my energy."

Keres kept himself from smiling at her fury. He'd discovered with his first mate that females did not welcome amusement at the wrong time. "Would you like me to go grab carry out for dinner, honey?"

"Why don't you go do that, stud muffin?" she growled at him. Rimi took her eyes off him to glance down at the hand she rubbed furiously against her jeans. "What did you do to my hand?"

"Stud muffin? Thanks," Keres answered cheerfully. He felt better than he had in months. The darkness had eliminated all joy and playfulness. This crystal dragon illuminated the shadows inside him. "What's wrong with your hand?"

When he reached for her wrist, she snatched her arm away. Of course, he had to reclaim it. This time, she gave up after a few seconds of struggle. He really was going to have to get her some food.

Her palm was unhurt. Keres turned her hand over and stared. There, on the back of her hand, as plain as day, lay an outline of a dragon. The sign of a mate bond. He'd felt the jolt as well when they'd touched. Keres looked at his hand. The skin was red but free of any distinguishable mark.

"We're mated," he said, incredulous.

"You have lost your mind. Dragons mate with humans—not other dragons. Well, that's how it goes for male dragons. Females are just screwed. Literally and figuratively."

"How many female dragons have you met?"

"My mother, obviously."

"What happened to her? Oldrik never said."

"She's gone now. I felt her pass from this life several centuries ago. We had a close connection."

"Why didn't you stay together?" Keres studied her beautiful face, unable to tear his gaze from her.

"As soon as Oldrik and I could survive, she left. Supposedly, we were safer without her. Dragons would soon search for her again. You know, the ones losing their grip on reality like you. Most would simply eliminate those competing for a mother's attention."

"Do you remember? Did she have a mark on her hand?" He brushed his fingers over the raised shape on her hand. A rush of arousal flooded through him. Keres stiffened his spine to keep from drawing her close.

"Stop touching me. It's making me crazy."

Keres stared at her before demanding, "How?"

"None of your business. Let go." Rimi tugged at her hand before giving up and glaring at him. "Fine. Hold my hand." She muttered, "Big bully" under her breath.

To Keres' surprise, he wanted her to like him. Mentally, he shook himself. He never felt bad about doing what he wanted. Well, at least when he was mateless. He'd cared about a lot of things in the past when he'd had someone who needed his care.

"Me too," burst from his lips. "It makes me crazy too."

Rimi stared at him. "It turns you on when you touch my hand?"

"Yes."

Keres moved closer, holding her gaze. He backed her up against the rocky wall and lowered his lips to hers. Instant heat flared between them—hot and erotic. His shaft hardened and pressed against the suddenly too tight fabric.

The enticing scent that had drawn him in wrapped around him as her body flooded with arousal. Keres wrapped his hand around the back of her neck, holding her close as he devoured her lips. He couldn't get close enough. Under his fingertips, he could detect her pulse racing as fast as his own.

Her lips softened, and she returned his kiss eagerly. Rimi wrapped her arms around his neck, clinging to Keres. She hummed with excitement and arousal.

Yet underneath all the passion, her body's dangerous status reverberated inside him as well. Keres ripped his mouth from hers and fought to regain control. Each of his senses screamed at him to ignore his concern and bask in the treasure he had discovered.

Unfortunately, they also told him she was dangerously weak. Her muscles trembled against him. Under her potent scent lay the hint of low blood sugar from lack of food. He needed to feed her before taxing her system anymore.

"Let's go hunt together. You need nourishment," he told her.

"I can't. I'm too weak," she admitted.

"I won't be able to leave you here. The mate bond won't allow it." Keres stepped a few feet away from her to test it, and she cried out in distress.

"Keres!" she cried and rushed forward to press herself into his arms.

"You'll have to ride me in human form. Can you hold on?"

"You're really going to take me for food?"

"Yes. If you die from hunger, you'll do me no good."

Shaking her head, Rimi snarled, "Of course. And here I thought you might be a nice guy. I should have known better. I'll hold on, because I have to."

Keres stifled a laugh at the thought that he, the black

dragon, was Mr. Nice Guy. "Stay close as I change. Then you can climb on my back."

In a few moments, Keres launched himself into the air. Rimi slipped to the left and then regained her balance. He suspected pure determination kept her in place. She was dangerously close to being too weak to ride. He could carry her in his claws, but that would diminish his ability to fend off an attack. Keres sent her energy through their fledgling bond. The channel between them wouldn't snap fully into effect until they mated.

Is this what it's like to be a male dragon? Having the ability to fly in any direction without fear?

Her question wasn't designed to make him ashamed of his sex, but it did. He could sense her joy at the sensation of the wind on her face and the smell of fresh flowers and nature. And this was in human form. How had her dragon survived without this freedom?

He flew back the way he had come, picturing an enormous field with animals he'd passed earlier. It was farther than he remembered it. Rimi rested her head on his neck and fell asleep. Her arms relaxed around his neck. Keres carefully balanced his precious cargo.

When the field came into view, he called her. *Rimi. Rimi, you have to wake up. Hold on, Mate.*

Her arms tightened around his neck, to his relief. Keres swooped and collected two cows, dispatching them quickly with a snap of his claws. He retreated to the edge of the pasture to drop them away from the herd before landing.

Rimi. You must change to eat.

I don't think I can, Keres.

Change now, Rimi. Otherwise, I will roast steaks here and force feed them to you. You must eat.

He supported her with the tip of one wing as she slid to the ground. Sending her strength, Keres pushed her shift. It was excruciating to watch as her shifter side battled for control. Finally, the crystal dragon stood next to him, shivering with exhaustion.

Keres ripped off a portion of the cow and held it to her snout. *Eat, Mate.* He almost lost a claw. Grinning, he pulled the rest of the carcass toward her. The crunching enthusiasm of her hunger reassured Keres she'd be okay.

When she'd finished the two, Rimi shook her head. *Sorry. I didn't offer to share.*

I'm good, Snowflake. Want another?

Snowflake?

That's what you remind me of. Beautifully unique with a sparkling shimmer and sharp edges.

Not cold and wet?

Was she teasing him? Keres liked it—a lot. *Never! Now, are you still hungry?*

No. I've been out here for too long. Someone will see me.

Anger rushed through him. *No one will ever threaten you again.*

Rimi brushed her snout against his to soothe Keres. *Take me home, Keres.*

He nodded. *Do you want to fly or would you rather ride?*

Ride, please.

With a shimmer, she morphed into her human form and scrambled onto his back. Keres was selfishly glad she'd chosen that option. He enjoyed having her wrapped around him, even if her shirt had regenerated around her when she shifted. His mate was indescribably alluring. He took to the sky and headed back toward her mountain.

He could feel the need building inside him. They would need to consummate the mate bond soon. Rimi's stamina and strength rebounded slowly with each moment that passed. He could wait until she was less fragile.

Mate? Would you send Oldrik a message? Tell him I'm with you and you're good? He was worried about you.

A blast of heat sizzled past Keres. Without a second's delay, he raised a wing to shield Rimi as he scanned for whoever had endangered his mate. There. He angled himself to guard his mate as he spotted a red dragon approaching. *Flatten yourself to me and hold on!*

Fury lanced through Keres at the insult. Who thought they could best him? He screamed his anger into the darkness, warning their attacker.

Keres! I'm afraid I'll fall.

His mate wasn't at a quarter of her strength yet. He would have to take shelter and protect her until she was well. Keres spat flames toward the invader as he flew toward her cave. Swerving and dodging the aggressive dragon's attack, Keres balanced his efforts with her ability to cling to him. When the cave opening loomed in front of him, Keres tucked his wings in close to his body and dove.

He spotted the flare of a second attacker's blast with barely enough time to roll to protect Rimi. The flames raked his underbelly. He roared at the offense, but Rimi's hold loosened. Keres dropped like a rock through the air to get below her and caught his mate between his wings like he'd performed that dangerous move a dozen times before.

Her breath jetted from her lungs at the impact, but Rimi immediately grabbed his scales with determination. *Go, Keres! I won't let go again.*

He spun around the mountain in an upward spiral that surprised the two opposing dragons. As Keres approached the mouth of Rimi's cave, he scanned the interior to make sure no one lurked inside. It was risky to take the time to investigate, but her entrance was a narrow tunnel. Someone lying in wait would have the advantage.

Again, he shielded Rimi from flames thrown at her. He understood the duo attacking him. He was an invading dragon. But why were they attacking her?

Pushing the question out of his mind, Keres dove into the entrance. Thrashing his tail to cause an avalanche, he sealed the opening behind them and skidded to a stop. The roars of the two thwarted dragons reached his ears, even through the layers of stone. It appeared he'd made a couple of enemies.

"What have you done?" Rimi asked, sliding off his back as quickly as possible.

Kept you safe? Keres suggested before shifting.

"How are we going to get out of here?"

"How about if we worry about that later? You need rest. I made sure you could get some." Keres crossed the short distance she'd put between them. The mate bond hadn't allowed her to stray far.

Scooping Rimi up in his arms, he carried her back to the large chamber. "Where do you sleep, Mate?"

"Pick a rock. Any rock," she said in a tone that told him how crappy her existence was. Her tone was markedly hopeless for anything different.

Spotting a patch of moss growing at the side of the cavern, Keres set her down close before stripping off his shirt. He draped it over the slight padding and unfastened his pants. Rimi whirled around to face the rock.

"Whoa! I'm not having sex with you."

"You will, but not now. Now, you'll rest. I'm only making a mattress for you."

"I'm not undressing."

"We'll take care of that when you're ready." He hid his

amusement at her harrumph of disbelief as he finished smoothing out his discarded apparel.

When he was naked, he helped her settle on top of his clothes and lowered himself to her side. Snuggling in next to her, Keres held her to his side. Her tense muscles were rigid against him.

"Sleep, Mate. I won't ravish you while you rest."

"You'll ravish me later?" she asked sarcastically.

"Exactly."

After a few moments, she softened in his arms. Exhaustion overwhelmed her ability to stay awake. Keres was confident that somewhere inside, she understood she was safe. He listened carefully as the dragons continued to rally outside the collapsed entrance. His mate would be safe. Keres would make sure of that.

Chapter 3

Finally, silence filled the interior space. The rampaging dragons had battered the entrance throughout the night before finally giving up. Rimi had slept through all but the very beginning of it.

Keres suspected that after they hadn't found a way inside easily, they had created as much destruction and havoc as possible. It made sense to him that someone so desperate to get to a female dragon would respond with spite when finding themselves blocked by another. Had they worked together to entomb Keres and Rimi inside the mountain?

He planned to wait until Rimi awoke and then search for a way out. At the moment, there was plenty of oxygen. His mate had eaten. They had water from the nearby spring-fed pool. And he held her in his arms. Keres pressed a kiss to her temple and loved how she squirmed closer with a slight smile as she slept. He'd given up on having this again. Keres vowed to treasure every moment.

Suspecting Rimi had not contacted Oldrik, he reached out. *Oldrik. I found her. She's not in the best shape but has now eaten and is sleeping. Rimi will contact you when she wakes up.* The distance would delay the message, but he'd hear back soon.

Not in the best shape? Blasted into his mind a short time later. *What's wrong with her?*

She's been trapped inside her refuge without food for too long. I'll keep her safe now.

You'll keep her safe?

Keres could hear the incredulity in Oldrik's message. *Yes. I'll keep her safe.*

How's your mind, Keres? That message was blunt.

Don't worry, Oldrik. I won't harm your sister. Keres had decided to wait until the mate bond had locked fully into place to reveal their connection. Oldrik would worry that Keres had invented that in his previous mental state.

You'll have her message me?

Absolutely.

Keres disconnected the link and closed his eyes. He would rest now with his mate. He also had missed sleep in recent weeks.

Rimi's arm crashed into his chin. Keres caught the next flailing strike and pinned her arms to her torso as she shook. She wasn't doing this deliberately. Something was seriously wrong. Adrenaline flooded through his body.

"Rimi! Wake up!"

She didn't respond, but continued to jerk. Unsure what to do, Keres pulled her away from the cavern wall to prevent her from striking it. After wadding up his shirt to put under her head, he forced himself to talk quietly and calmly. "Rimi? Are you hurt? What's happening?"

Her eyes opened to meet his. Keres's heart lurched at the fear glistening in her gaze. He would do anything to keep her from being frightened like this. When her beautiful green eyes rolled back into her head, he smoothed her hair away from her face and reassured her.

"You're okay, Snowflake. I'm here with you. This will pass soon." He rested his hand on her forehead and felt himself yanked into the chaos inside her brain. Immediately, he started looking around for some way to help her. Instead of threads of light zipping through the darkness, the connections in her brain were clumped together like massive traffic jams.

There! Keres approached a tangle of crystal white strands of light. Placing his fingers on one thread, he winced and pulled away as an electric charge burst through him like he'd touched live wires. *Buck up, black dragon. You've got extra fire protection for a reason.*

Concentrating, Keres forced the thin scales that formed his human-like skin to thicken slightly. He couldn't interfere with his dexterity. That snarl of strands would take finessing. But he'd have to hold on to the lines to untangle them.

Taking a deep breath, he filled his mind with reassurances as he worked to straighten out the threads of crystal light. Keres wasn't sure who he tried to encourage most with the mental messages—himself or Rimi. He just hoped unraveling the clusters worked.

He couldn't rush. Snapping one of these lines would have disastrous effects. This reminded him of a bunch of necklaces he'd found in a treasure chest eons ago. The pirate must have tossed the mass of gold chains in with a curse, unwilling to take the time to separate them.

Keres had taken it as a challenge and had worked on it for several years, freeing one after another. He did the same delicate work, but on a faster time frame. As each strand of sparkling white light slipped away from the others, Rimi relaxed infinitesimally.

Sorry, Mate. I'm a bit fumble-fingered here. Breathe slowly, Rimi. We can figure this out.

His eyesight was blurry as the last two slid away from each other. Keres forced himself to scan despite the fog clouding his tired eyes to make sure he didn't spot another problem in the darkness of her mind. Threads of all colors zipped past him in energetic, unobstructed lines. The beauty of her thoughts mesmerized him.

Her hand wrapped around his on her forehead. Keres pulled himself away and looked down at her gorgeous face. "Rimi? How do you feel?"

"Like I ran a marathon through electric eel infested water," she answered wearily.

He chuckled at that visual image. "Understandable. Close your eyes, Rimi. You should sleep easier now."

Rimi nodded and closed her eyes. She was asleep in seconds. Keres listened to her breathing as he settled back down beside her and drew her back to his chest. To his delight, Rimi sighed happily and patted his stomach.

When he heard her slight snore, Keres allowed himself to press a kiss to her temple and inhaled her scent. Keres would never get enough of the essence that had first drawn him close. Closing his bleary eyes, he relaxed for the first time in months. Rimi would be okay now.

🐫 🐫 🐫

Soft lips nibbled a tantalizing line down the cord of his neck. Keres lifted a hand to thread his fingers through her silky white hair. He hummed his enjoyment of her attention. "Snowflake," he whispered.

"Can we forget who we are? And just...?"

Growling, Keres rolled her onto her back. When the loose stones poked into his arm, he changed directions, hauling her on top of his naked body. His hand tangled in Rimi's hair to guide her mouth to his. Instant fire erupted between them as he tasted her delicious flavor. He'd never get enough of her. The knowledge that Rimi had saved him from the brink of a horrendous fate blended with the desire that burned inside him. She would always mean more than everything to him.

He ripped his mouth away from hers, forcing himself to slow down. "Rimi, are you ready for this?"

"I don't have a clue," she whispered before adding, "but I ache for you. No one else."

A rumble escaped from his throat at the thought of anyone else ever touching her. She tugged at his hair, bringing his attention back to the present as she slid her tongue into his mouth to meet his. Her kisses were eager but unpracticed. Keres loved the slight awkwardness of the exchange as she bumped noses with him.

She lifted her lips slightly from his and snapped, "Stop projecting conquering thoughts. We both know I've never done this for obvious reasons. How about replacing those with 'don't screw this up' worries?"

He smirked and then felt the concern she tried to hide under bravado. She was worried she'd disappoint him. That could never happen. "I'll do my best, Mate."

"Good," she muttered, and when he cupped her breast and flicked his thumb across her erect nipple, she moaned.

Keres loved watching her reaction to his caresses. He grabbed the front of her shirt and ripped it off, pressing a kiss to that almost healed spot over her heart. He could have lost this. Lost her.

She arched her back, pushing her sweet tits toward him.

Keres rewarded her by curling up to capture one impudent peak and pulled it deep into his mouth to tease with his tongue. Her moan of delight went straight to his cock.

Her denim-covered legs eased to the side of his hips, allowing her to rub her mound against his shaft. Those jeans needed to go. Keres wrapped his hands around her waist and lifted her torso to sit her up, allowing him to access the front of her jeans.

Rimi stared at his chest before reaching forward to trace the muscles as he unfastened her waistband and drew the zipper down. Each inch of her delicious form he revealed pushed his arousal higher. This was taking too long. Keres shifted a fingertip into a talon on each hand and sliced through the heavy material. When she rose onto her knees in surprise, he whisked the material away.

"Commando. I love it." He growled at the sight of the silky curls between her legs.

"It's not like I can go lingerie shopping."

"You don't need lace, Snowflake, to capture my attention," he assured her while noting the need to lavish his mate with beautiful underthings. All girls liked to play dress up, didn't they?

She looked at him as if she could follow his thoughts. Keres quickly distracted her. He ran his once-again fingertip over her hipbone to trace the cleft of her lower lips. Her pussy was slick with arousal, coating his skin.

He held her gaze as he lifted his hand to his lips and licked her juice from his finger. Her eyes widened as she watched his reaction. "Mmm." He hummed his enjoyment. "I think I need another taste."

Before she could react, he helped her settle back onto his clothes that formed that makeshift mattress. Keres pressed his lips to hers, exploring her mouth until they were both panting with need. He loved how she challenged his control, meeting every exchange with heat.

He kissed a path down her throat, memorizing every sensitive spot he discovered. Pausing, Keres propped himself up on one forearm to stare down at the desire written on her face. She wanted him as much as he craved her beautiful body.

"You take my breath away, Snowflake."

He drew his fingers over her collarbone as he admired her curves. "I was not expecting you. Best surprise ever." Cupping one breast in his hand, Keres leaned down to taste her nipple. Drawing it into his mouth, he swirled his tongue around the taut peak before biting it lightly.

At the slight taste of pain, Rimi inhaled sharply and dug her fingernails slightly into his shoulders. Her delicious scent increased as she rubbed her mound against his hard thigh separating hers. Keres smiled against her skin. He loved discovering her secrets. His mate had enjoyed that sting.

Once he released the tight peak with a pop, Keres kissed and nibbled the under portion of her breast, allowing his beard to caress her as well. Rimi's eager movements against him urged Keres on, but he planned on taking his time. At least as long as he could stay in control.

After giving attention to her other breast, Keres drew a line down her abdomen to those silky blonde curls with his mouth. He kissed the top of her mound before tracing the cleft with his tongue. When she moved her legs apart, silently requesting intimate attention, he rewarded her by exploring her pink folds.

Stroking his hand down the inside of her thigh, Keres spread her legs wide. The alluring buffet before him was impossible to resist. He brushed his mustache lightly over her clit as he sampled her sweet juices. She shivered and lifted her hips higher to entice him.

Keres answered her need. He swirled his tongue around

her clit before drawing it gently into his mouth. She froze under him. Her pulse raced under his palm on her inner thigh. She was so close.

"Mmmm." He hummed his enjoyment against her pussy as he slowly pressed two fingers deep into her.

A low keening sound tumbled from her lips before she screamed, "Keres!" into the cavern. As that sound reverberated under the domed ceiling, Keres thrashed his tongue across her sensitive bundle of nerves and stretched her tight passage with his fingers.

Her fingers bit into his shoulders. "Too much!" she whispered.

"No, Snowflake. There's never too much bliss. Come again for me."

She shook her head as if his request was impossible. Keres accepted the challenge and lowered his mouth to her once again. Her next scream sounded slightly hoarse. Keres realized she didn't have the chance to even talk. This definitely taxed her vocal cords.

He gentled his caress, extending her second orgasm as long as possible as he prepared her to take him. When he finally lifted his head, Rimi sagged against the slight padding. Keres rose to his hands and knees and prowled over her, caging her tantalizing form under him.

After kissing her hard once to allow her to taste herself on his lips, Keres lifted his head and met her dazed gaze. "Mine."

Rimi didn't try to deny their connection. "Yours."

Keres lowered his hips between her widely spread thighs and fit himself to her drenched opening. The lingering contractions from her last orgasm squeezed the head of his cock. Holding himself back from plunging forward with iron-clad control, Keres pressed himself slowly into her heat. She was so tight he struggled to hold it together. Gritting his teeth, Keres counted by sevens.

When he pressed deep inside her, an explosion in his mind rocked Keres. He looked at Rimi to make sure she was okay. Her shocked expression told him the mate bond affected her strongly as it locked into place. He withdrew and filled her again. Pleasure replaced the surprise on her face.

"Now the fun begins, Snowflake. Hold on. You feel incredible around me."

Keres concentrated on her pleasure, stroking and caressing her beautiful curves. She moved with him tentatively, but with growing confidence as he praised her. Their lovemaking had an edge to it he'd never felt before. Like being buried inside her was exactly where he needed to be.

He slid a hand between their bodies to brush a fingertip over her clit. The extra stimulation pushed Rimi into a massive orgasm. Her tight passage clamped around him. Each pulse of pleasure threatened his control.

Keres wasn't ready for this to end. He gritted his teeth together and slowed his thrusts to draw out her climax before slowly building the sensations back to a boiling point. Their bodies slid together as heat built inside the cavern. Her pale skin glowed in the light of the torches, making him wish to both ravish Rimi and protect her at the same time.

Her hands caressed down his spine to grip his butt as she rose to meet him. "Find your pleasure with me, Keres," she demanded, squeezing her inner muscles in a move so irresistible he couldn't refuse.

Powering deeply into her, Keres ground against her most sensitive places. He controlled his climax by sheer force until he felt hers begin. Then he allowed himself to follow her. His heart beat wildly like it would explode as he filled her.

Gathering Rimi against him, Keres rolled her back onto his clothing. Her soft kiss to his lips melted any lingering doubts or reserve. Keres cut off the shouted questions that echoed in his mind. His horde could wait.

He focused completely on caring for his mate.

Chapter 4

Waking up in a dragon shifter's arms after being entombed in a cave was not on Rimi's bucket list—even if she felt incredible. Who knew mating would be like that? She guessed the mate bond snapping into place had caused the riot of sensations inside her. Well, other than the pleasure Keres had lavished on her. She'd always feared sex. Keres had shown her how incredible making love could be.

"You're concentrating too hard, Snowflake." His growly, rough morning voice sent shivers through her.

"You can't hear what I'm thinking, can you?"

"Only if you're on loud announcement mode or talking to me privately. I can sense that you are feeling well this morning."

"How do we know if it's morning?" she asked, waving a hand at the darkened chamber.

"Internal clock," he answered. "Let's get cleaned up and then we'll figure out how to dig out of here."

"I've never found another opening."

"Baths first. Escape second," he suggested.

"I guess dying covered in sex juice is not the thing to do," she scoffed.

"Sex juice? I love it," he said with a chuckle, diffusing her frustration. Keres lifted his hand and placed a kiss on the now-visible dragon shape decorating it.

A thrill shimmied down her back. Rimi shouldn't feel that, but she did. Unable to resist, she lifted her hand and licked the symbol now marked on the back. His low groan made her clench her thighs together. She had heard that sound before, when he'd pressed himself deep inside her.

Rimi tried to pull herself together. His soft chuckle told her he knew exactly how much he affected her. "Okay. Baths first."

"Good idea." Moving smoothly, Keres rose to his feet. He reached down and easily pulled Rimi to her feet.

She hated to admit how much she loved his strength. Because of her need to hide, Rimi couldn't glide around the sky, building muscles. She was round and soft, not all hard angles and chiseled physique like Keres. Her gaze dropped to his butt. *Damn.*

He looked like the movie stars she'd studied in abandoned magazines. Handsome, powerful, and magnetic. His black hair was tousled and unkept—a sign of his decline in the last months. Her fingers itched to brush it away from his mesmerizing eyes before tasting every inch of her mate's delicious form.

"Thank you, Mate. I like everything about you, too."

"Stop eavesdropping on my thoughts," she snapped.

"Remember, I'll hear everything you broadcast. You'll get used to it. Besides, you can ogle my ass anytime. Or really, any part of me."

Rimi rolled her eyes so hard she could almost hear them rattle. Like she wanted to check out his assets. She fought with herself to keep her focus on his broad shoulders as he waded into the water until he was waist deep. Breathing a sigh of relief, she stepped into the natural pool as well.

Turning to float on her back, Rimi savored the cool liquid on her skin. The waterhole had quickly become the only positive feature in this cavern. She'd wanted to search for another place but had spotted those dragons a week ago. When they hadn't moved on, she was stuck.

Thank goodness the swinging blade had discouraged them. When the bravest had entered the narrow opening first, that booby trap had taken him out. The remaining two hadn't dared enter after that, thank goodness. It had taken days of hauling water to pour over the stones inside to wash away the stench of the slain dragon's blood after she'd pushed the body out.

Hands wrapped under her, helping Rimi float on the surface. Keres pressed a kiss to her shoulder before straightening. He didn't say a word, but simply held her.

To her dismay, tears poured from her eyes. Her entire life, no one had been there to help her. Her mom had abandoned her and her twin, Oldrik, as soon as he could forage for the two of them. Oldrik had protected her until he'd matured. The need for a mate had driven him to leave. He hadn't gone willingly and had tried to convince her to come with him. Her mother had pounded into her brain the need to hide from male dragons. The idea of having a horde of dragons around her had terrified Rimi, so she'd refused. After he left, she'd felt so alone.

Keres lifted her into his arms. He hugged her tight to his chest as he brushed his fingers over her scalp and through her locks. She curled herself around him, yielding to the need for support. She could be weak for a bit.

"You are the bravest dragon I've ever met," Keres whispered to her. "You will never be alone again."

"Great luck I have. We're trapped in here and will die. The

last surviving one of us will turn to cannibalism to survive," she muttered, imagining the worst-case scenario.

"Remember, bath first. Get out second." His hands splashed water over her gently.

"I can get cleaned up," she protested, shifting away slightly.

"You can," he acknowledged as he continued to stroke wet hands over her.

"That means you can stop."

His hands froze on her hips. "Do you not like my touch, Mate?"

She opened her mouth to tell him no, but as she met his gaze, she noticed his eyes had turned completely black. He seemed to see inside her soul. Rimi nodded. "I love the way you touch me."

"Then letting me take care of you makes us both happy." He returned his attention back to his task.

Two could play at that game. Rimi splashed water onto his chest and smoothed the liquid over his skin. How could anyone be in that incredible shape? His muscles felt like they had muscles. When she reached below the waterline, her fingers brushed his rigid shaft. Her gaze jolted upward to meet his as her fingers wrapped around him. That had fit inside her?

"If we are close, Snowflake, my cock is going to celebrate," he told her with a smirk that she wanted to not like, but it was so darn cute.

He wrapped his hand around hers and guided her grip up and down his cock. "We will have a lifetime to share what excites us."

"You like this," Rimi whispered before she could stop herself.

"Yes," he growled, easily revealing how much the caress meant.

She was disappointed when he drew her hand away, "But..."

"We need to figure out how to get out of here, Snowflake. Then we can play all we wish."

Rimi nodded. He was right. "What happens if we get out and those two are still outside?"

"They die if they attack my mate. I don't know if they'll detect that we're mated—or if they'll care. This is unfamiliar territory for me as well. You will be safe, and we'll head home."

That term home seemed so alien. She'd never had a home. Only temporary shelter.

"You have a home, Mate, with me."

"Stop reading my mind," she snapped. It was disconcerting to have him pick up on her feelings so easily.

"I didn't need to snoop in on your thoughts, Rimi. Your expression and the small bit of your history that I know clued me in on that one."

"Do you really want to battle other dragons who want to mate with me?" She gasped when his hands tightened painfully on her hips.

"No one will mate with you. You are mine. No one else's." Keres claimed her with such a fierce look and tone that she shivered in reaction.

Rimi definitely didn't want to tangle with him. Unfortunately, he had to understand her reality. "Keres, listen to me. Female dragons are rare. I don't think nature is going to let you keep me."

"It is. Nature doesn't get a choice here. You are mine," he repeated.

Shaking her head, Rimi stopped arguing with him. He seemed so sure. Could their mating have changed her allure for others? That little voice in the back of her mind asked if it would make her more appealing to steal away or less since she belonged to Keres?

"Save yourself if there is a conflict. A male dragon won't hurt me. Well, not to the point I couldn't try to produce an heir."

She forced herself to stop talking when Keres's intensive glower brought his brows almost together in the middle of his forehead. "I get it. I'm yours."

"Good girl."

She didn't understand the thrill that went through her at the small bit of praise. Keres stepped forward to pull her through the darkly shadowed water. He hugged her tight against his hard muscles and dipped his head to capture her lips.

The kiss seared through her, staking his claim. She wrapped her arms around his neck and held on for dear life as he dominated her so deliciously. Her brain went on overload, unable to focus on anything else but him. Rimi panted when he lifted his head, as she struggled to pull her thoughts back together.

"Now. We'll figure a way out of here and start our way home."

"Can we stop and get more cows?" she blurted.

"Of course. Let's go see what those two disasters did to the entrance." Holding her hand, he helped her out of the pool.

Rimi treasured those small gestures. He didn't know he was her first for so many things. She squeezed his hand before letting go. Did his fingers linger against hers?

After checking out the amount of rubble filling the entrance, Rimi figured she needed to scout for another exit. Between Keres sealing the opening behind them and those two raging dragons, the passage appeared permanently sealed.

She'd already checked for a secondary way out when she'd settled here. After two months, she'd given up.

"Scoot back, Snowflake. I'm going to change and see if I can push some of these stones out."

Keres shifted effortlessly into his striking black dragon form. If anything could create an opening for them, it would be this massively muscled beast. Keres lowered his head to press against the rubble. Nothing moved. His talons dug into the stone floor of the cavern, and his muscles shook with the strain. Rimi didn't detect any movement at all.

Feeling ridiculous just watching, Rimi shifted as well. Squeezing her smaller bulk beside her enormous black mate, Rimi set her forehead against the stones and pushed. Again, nothing.

Fury filled her. She finally had a chance to live instead of hide. At least to share her life with someone, and now those rocks kept her trapped. This was completely unfair. She strained forward with everything inside her. When she considered giving up, a muffled tinkling of rocks falling drifted to her ears.

That's it, Mate. Push with me, Keres encouraged her.

Remembering how Keres dug his claws into the stone, Rimi pushed hers into the hard surface. Small stones skittered across the ground under their feet. She lined up shoulder to shoulder with her mate, and Keres's powerful muscles strained next to hers.

I'm trying.

That's it. The rock is moving, Keres announced.

The quiet dribble of rocks steadily increased to a torrent. How much would they have to move to create an opening? She backed up and lunged forward, hoping momentum would help clear the way.

That was it! Suddenly, Keres threw himself over her

vulnerable form. The impact knocked the air from her lungs. Rimi pushed at him desperately, trying to shove him off. She struggled to breathe, pinned under Keres's weight. What was he doing?

That thought had barely formed in her brain when enormous boulders rained down on top of Keres. He jolted into her. *Keres!*

She grabbed ahold of the foreleg closest to her and wiggled backward. Her muscles burned with the effort to move both of them away from the assault from above. Keres didn't yell at her. He didn't move.

Her heart leapt into her throat. He had to be okay. She heaved herself backward, yanking him to what she hoped was safety. Seconds later, a massive boulder crashed down on the space where their heads had been seconds before with a thunderous impact. The sliver of sunlight it revealed gave her hope that an escape was possible. A menacing rumble sounded above them, demanding her attention.

Keres! We have to move now!

His mind brushed hers, and she seized on it. *Help me, damn it!* She flung herself backward, dragging him with her, and felt Keres assisting her efforts. She rose as high as she could on her legs and threw herself backward with Keres' help.

A ton of rubble cascaded from the side of the mountain. The tumbling mass created a slanted platform, ushering the stone rock face past their location and down the slope. From their new location, she could see their former position had become the impact zone. As debris filled the air, Rimi hid her face against Keres's scales and held her breath.

The glint of sunlight ricocheting off Keres's pitch-black scales signaled it was safe to assess their situation. Motes of dust twinkled in the bright glare. Rimi dragged air into her starving lungs.

Keres

Keres? Are you okay?

Did you get bashed?

How could I? You threw yourself over me. How are you?

Ever wonder what one of those smashed hamburgers feels like?

I don't even know what that is! I'm shifting to check you out.

No! The roof is too heavily damaged. More could come down at any time. We need to get out of here. Can you lead the way?

Scared that more rocks would rain down on them, Rimi squeezed around him and stepped carefully to scale the rubble. When Keres didn't follow her, she glanced back at him. Both of his eyes were swollen shut. He could barely see, if at all. How could she get him out of here safely?

An idea popped into her mind. She swung her tail to brush his mouth. *Grab my tail. I'll tug you from the rubble.* Navigating over the shifting stones seemed to take forever, but soon, she reached a space where she could launch herself into the air.

Flapping her wings, she rose a few feet. *Keep coming, Keres. I'll tell you when to fly.*

The gusts of air from her wings shifted the rocks under his feet. Keres slid down the incline back into the cavern. *Push off now, Keres. Fly toward me.*

In a split second, he launched himself up into the air. A rattling avalanche of stone gained speed, sweeping everything in its path down the mountain and filling the area where she'd existed for so long. Rimi didn't have time to consider what had happened. She navigated higher, getting away from that mess, and Keres followed her.

That was probably not the best idea I've ever had, Keres announced wryly.

But it worked.

A blast of heat seared over Keres's damaged scales, making him whirl around.

Fuck my life! Rimi roared her indignation at the attack. It's the same dragon who knocked down the mountain.

Which direction, Rimi? I don't want to hurt you.

Five o'clock and nine o'clock. I'll stay on your right flank.

Which is larger?

Nine o'clock, she messaged.

The fiery torrent that emerged from Keres's mouth scared her. She knew he was powerful, but wow! Rimi automatically shied away from the heat before steeling her nerves to stay tucked in next to Keres' side. When the smaller dragon targeted her, Rimi reacted automatically and sent her own flames his way.

Pull a deep breath in from your abdomen, Keres instructed. *Kindle your flames and count to three. Then, fire.*

Frightened to the core, Rimi tried to follow his instructions. All her life she'd run and hidden. Perhaps thrown a warning shot over her shoulder as she ducked and weaved. She definitely had never learned to fight, but these dragons needed to leave them alone. How dare they bury them alive!

This time, the flames roared from her throat. Fear and fury combined. She recoiled at the ferocity of her attack. *Damn!* That worked. The red dragon distanced himself to stay out of range.

Careful, Keres! The bigger green dragon is changing angles. Think seven this time.

Following her instructions, Keres torched him again.

Bullseye! Rimi celebrated.

The attacking dragons hesitated. They lifted their snouts into the air. The larger one let out a roar and turned to flee. Immediately, the smaller one followed. Within seconds, they were specks on the horizon.

Tell me what's happening, mate!

They... They're gone. Incredulity flooded her. The dragons *had scented her and departed. Could she actually be safe as Keres's mate?*

Good. Can you guide me to a stream or lake? I think if I wash my eyes out, I'll be able to see.

In a short time, Rimi stood next to a creek bed as the black dragon splashed in the water. He lifted his head from the cool liquid and turned to assess her condition. *That's better. I can see more clearly. Come in. Your scales are more gray than crystal. Between the two of us, we've brought half the mountain peak down.*

Rimi stared at him, speechless. How could he be so nonchalant? Entombed. Cavern collapse. Keres hurt. Dragon attack. Her body shook as all the events of the last few hours registered. She shifted from dragon to human as she trembled.

Strong arms wrapped around her. Rimi glanced up to see Keres's dark eyes filled with concern. The mesmerizing, dark orbs were now bloodshot and bleary.

"Sorry. It must be a reaction," she whispered.

"You have nothing to apologize for, Snowflake. I definitely needed a hug as well. Life is definitely not boring with you, Mate."

She tilted her head as she stared at him. Was he being serious or sarcastic? The corner of his mouth twitched, and Rimi knew he was trying not to laugh. She shook her head. "I could do with some boredom."

"Let's get cleaned up, go grab something to eat, and get out of here."

Rimi nodded. "I'd love to get far away from here."

She allowed him to scoop her up and carry her into the creek. Even though shifting had dispersed most of the dirt, Rimi felt better with her hair and skin rinsed. When he finished helping her, Keres attended to his own bath.

Rimi bit her lip. His skin was a quilt of bruises and scorch marks. She stepped toward him to help. Pressing her hand lightly to his ribs, Rimi whispered, "You could have died. Why did you cover me?"

"You're too pretty to bruise. The colors will fade quickly. Dragons heal rapidly."

The skin under her hand morphed to his normal skin color. Keres groaned. "That's better. Those broken ribs were killing me."

Moving her hand to another purple bruise, she heard him groan in relief. She tilted her hand to peek underneath. Unblemished skin. "That can't be happening."

"Try it again. Press your palm here. The back of my neck got sizzled." When her cool fingers wrapped around the area, Keres smiled. "So, healing is a crystal dragon's special talent?"

"I don't know, Keres. I'm never sick. Let's try more places." She scanned his battered form. "This is going to take a while."

"Damn, Mate. I can't wait to have your hands around my cock."

"Keres!" she said as her face heated with embarrassment. Thank goodness she was behind him. And that the next bruise she had to target was on his firm butt....

Chapter 5

Rimi was completely exhausted—mentally and physically—at the end of their third day of travel. Being out in the open had her on edge every second of the day. She definitely didn't sleep well, even with a black dragon guarding her. Keres pushed her as hard as he could, but his mate's welfare was his priority.

Keres broke up the trip to his mountain into chunks with frequent rest breaks. His mate was not accustomed to flying long distances, only short bursts. When she grew too tired, he would have her shift and ride on his back. Despite the hard voyage, he loved having her only to himself.

Twice they ran into other dragons. Once a group of three appeared downwind of him and Rimi on the horizon. They changed course to intercept them. Keres' concern flipped to confusion when they suddenly veered off-course. The second time, it was a solitary, young, green dragon. Keres had known he could take one easily, even protecting Rimi. Again, after getting within a couple of miles, the potential opponent turned and ran.

On the afternoon of their third day, they finally flew over the border of Wyvern. Keres sent a message to the horde.

I've returned. Did you give my mountain away? That, of course, could never happen until a full year passed. There were too many safeguards around Keres' treasures, and his staff was too loyal to enable anyone to take over his possessions.

Keres? Drake's message reverberated in his mind.

And Rimi. His mate's voice spoke through the link with his horde.

Keres shook his head. He should have anticipated that Rimi would overhear the conversation. His mate's mental voice sounded weak. He needed to get her home.

Everyone, meet Rimi. My mate. She's a crystal dragon.

A million questions pelted their way. One voice stood out from everyone's.

Oldrik demanded, sounding incredulous. *Rimi?*

Oldrik, I can't wait to see you. I'm sorry I didn't contact you before. We were busy. Her voice was weak, and Keres stepped in to stop any plans before they could be made.

Everyone will have to wait. My mate needs rest. Give us three days and then we'll gather, Keres stated firmly. *Oldrik, you may visit in two days.*

Keres? Are you... okay? Drake asked.

Better than okay, Keres stated firmly. He shut off the rest of the questions coming to himself or Rimi. The horde knew they were in Wyvern and that his mental status had regained its balance. That was all that mattered now.

We're almost to my mountain, Rimi. It's there, ahead of us.

The one with the black rocks? She hesitated for several long seconds before admitting, *I don't think I'm ready to go back into a cavern, Keres.*

Then, we'll go into my home and explore my lair later.

Her relief flooded through their mental connection as she relaxed against his scales. Pleased she'd finally shared her worries, he rewarded her by altering their path slightly so she could catch glimpses of his mansion. The monumental building with marble columns stood out pristinely white against the green lawn and black rocks that wrapped around it.

Wow! That's impressive. I bet it seemed almost magical when lights illuminated the front at night.

I think you will be comfortable here. A soak in a hot tub would soothe your muscles. Would you rather eat or bathe first?

I'm starving, but getting clean sounds like a dream.

Then our priority will be to get rid of the road dirt. While we do that, my chef will prepare a light dinner for us before bed.

You'll have staff there? You didn't plan to return, did you?

My staff is very loyal. They chose to continue as if I would be home at any moment.

Meeting them will be a pleasure.

Tomorrow, Snowflake.

She nodded against his scales. She was too tired to argue with him. Rimi wouldn't be this easy to guide after a couple days of sleep and good nutrition. Keres would know when she felt better as her fire returned.

He circled over the mansion and trumpeted his return. His staff ran out of the house and barn to wave and clap. Keres tamped down his pleasure at seeing them. As Rimi had guessed, he hadn't planned to come back. Many of his staff had been with him for years and most for generations of their families.

You were worried about them, Rimi guessed, picking up on his emotions.

None of that matters now, Mate. I found you and we have returned. He changed the subject to distract her. *How excited do you think they will be to discover they now have two dragons on the mountain?*

I hope they like me.

Her quiet, worried voice went straight to his heart. *They will love you, Snowflake. How could they not?*

By the time he landed, his staff had gathered around the front lawn. Keres waited for Rimi to slide from his back before changing. He wrapped an arm around her waist and escorted her closer.

"Thank you for the warm welcome. It is my pleasure to introduce you to..."

Before he could add Rimi's name, scattered people through the crowd dropped to their knees, grinning and nudging their neighbors to do the same. "Dragon. She's a dragon," circulated through those assembled.

Keres glanced at Rimi and smiled at the awe-inspiring sight. She was glowing. Her nervousness in meeting his staff had sparked her dragon side to reveal itself. She stood in human form, but no one could mistake the powerful, sparkling aura that surrounded Rimi.

He cleared his throat and started again. "It is my pleasure to introduce you to my mate, Rimi, a crystal dragon. I trust you will care for her as you have tended me through so many years."

An ear-shattering roar of excitement burst through the crowd before shouted greetings of "Welcome," and "Long live Rimi," echoed through the air.

Squeezing her tight against his side, Keres whispered, "I think they're glad to meet you, Snowflake."

He turned to the crowd and announced, "It has been a long journey, and my mate is tired. I will insist she rest before meeting everyone."

Applause followed, signaling their approval of his protectiveness.

Nodding his thanks at their understanding, Keres swept Rimi into his arms and carried her forward. The crowd parted to allow them to pass, and his butler opened the door.

"Thank you, Russell," Keres told the long-time employee. His joy at speaking again to his butler didn't surprise him. Leaving home and his people had torn him apart inside.

"My pleasure, sir. And ma'am. Welcome home," Russell said with a smile.

"I'm glad to meet you, Russell," Rimi called over Keres's shoulder as he entered.

"Could you have a light dinner brought to our room in an hour?" Keres requested.

"Yes, sir. The rooms were refreshed today."

"Thank you, Russell." His butler had always amazed him with his ability to anticipate whatever was needed. How could he have known they were on their way? However Russell had predicted their arrival, he appreciated it.

"I could have talked to them," Rimi whispered when they reached a quiet hallway.

"Everyone understands I need to take care of my mate. They will meet you soon."

She dropped her head to his shoulder and relaxed in his arms. As he suspected, Rimi was exhausted. "Shower or bath, Snowflake?"

"I'd love to try a hot bath, but I'm afraid I'll fall asleep."

"Leave it to me, Rimi. I'll always take care of you."

Keres carried her into the large suite he'd occupied by himself since his last mate passed away a couple of centuries ago. He'd had the house remodeled over the years to create several chambers containing a bedroom and a vast attached bathroom. Each time he'd lost a mate, Keres had moved into a new room as he waited for his newest match to join him.

He scanned the room where he'd slowly descended into the darkness. The walls seemed to resonate with despair and negativity. Keres shook his head. He wouldn't expose Rimi to these black vibes. Turning, he carried her from that room and moved to the next.

"That was a nice room?" she said, a questioning lilt to her voice at the end.

"It is not the room for you. What is your favorite color, Rimi?"

"I love purple."

"We will share the lilac room," he told her and strode down the hall to the last room. There, he threw back the door and carried her across the threshold.

"Wow!"

Keres set Rimi's feet on the lush carpet in front of him and wrapped his arms around her waist to steady her. She leaned back against Keres's chest and checked out the space. He leaned slightly to the right to see her face.

"This room is gorgeous."

Keres nodded to himself. This was the right move. They needed a space of their own—far away from the anguish that had ruled his life for so long.

"I am glad you like it. I hope you will be happy here. If not, I'll rely on you to tell me what needs to change."

"O—Okay," she said hesitantly.

He would soften this request later, when they'd settled into the new space. "Come, Mate. Let's take a bath."

Rimi moaned in anticipation. "That sounds lovely." She slid her hand into Keres and followed him into the enormous bathroom. There, the lilac carpet changed to slate gray tiles with beautiful wallpaper of purple blossom clusters in all shades.

"I can't believe how lovely this room is. It's a totally different vibe than the other one," she said, glancing around. "Of course, I'm used to rocks and dark shadows."

"Your world has changed now, Rimi. This room does have a different mood. I plan to enjoy it with you."

Keres treasured the faint blush on her cheeks as she noticed the king-size bed. He would enjoy helping her experience luxuries. As his shaft responded to the mental picture of them tangled up together, Keres quickly finished the tour. "The toilet is through there. Would you like to use it before your bath?"

"Yes, please." She scurried to the small room and shut the door for privacy.

The right corner of his mouth turned up in a wry smile. Rimi would have many adjustments in her life ahead. Hopefully, she would be his mate for the rest of his life. He closed the bathroom door between the bathroom and bedroom.

Turning on the water, he fine-tuned the temperature, thanking the old system of heating water that his staff had reinstalled after everything using technology had failed. He poured a small amount of bath salts into the cascading water and sniffed in appreciation of the soft scent.

"That smells heavenly. I can't wait to get out of these clothes," Rimi announced, dragging her shirt over her head.

"Daddy's job," Keres told her, pulling the material from her hand and tossing it aside.

"Daddy?" she whispered.

"Yes, Snowflake. Have you heard of Daddy Doms?"

She shook her head so rapidly, he knew she was lying.

"Lying to your Daddy will earn you a spanking."

As if moving unintentionally, Rimi shielded her bottom with her hands.

"Come, Rimi. Let's get you in the tub."

He stepped forward and unzipped her low-slung jeans. Pushing them over her hips, he lowered himself to one knee to draw them down to her ankles. "Lift this foot," he said, tapping the toe of her right sneaker.

Rimi held onto his shoulders and shifted her weight to follow his directions. In a short time, he had her shoes and pants removed. Rising to his feet, Keres deliberately brushed his body against her curves. He wanted her to get used to being touched. She'd spent too much time alone and scared.

"Good girl. Let's get these off you," he suggested, running his index finger under her bra strap. He removed the plain garment before trailing his fingertips over her tummy.

"I'm sorry I don't have fancy underwear," she whispered.

"I don't need itchy lace to make me want you, Snowflake. However, I will be glad to collect some delicates for you if you'd like them," he assured her.

She hesitated briefly before nodding. "I'd love to have a fancy set."

"Then, I will make sure you have lingerie to wear."

Rimi had missed out on so much. He would do his best to provide anything she wished to try.

When she was completely nude, Keres helped Rimi into the tub. She settled into the fragrant water with a sigh of enjoyment and lowered her eyelids to savor the warmth. His turn. Keres pulled his T-shirt over his head. The rustle of his clothing must have reached Rimi, for she opened her eyes to glance at him. He loved how her eyes widened at the sight of his bare chest. Keres unfastened his jeans and thrust them to the ground to step out of his shoes and the denim fabric.

"You're going to join me?" she whispered.

"Of course. I don't want you to fall asleep and slide under the water. Scoot up a bit. I'll slip in behind you."

Soon, he cradled her safely against his chest, loving how she relaxed against him. Her eyes closed in obvious enjoyment. A quiet sound of movement whispered through the closed door between the two rooms. As Keres had anticipated, his staff had discovered he had changed rooms. They were efficiently shifting his belongings to this bedchamber and would leave clean clothing for Rimi as well.

She sat up slightly in alarm, glancing over her shoulder toward the bathroom door. "Who's out there?"

"My staff are simply bringing us some food and clothing. They will not come in here," Keres promised.

"Are you sure?" she asked.

"Would you walk into a room where two dragons bathed without permission?"

She looked at him in shock before shaking her head. "No way."

"Neither will they. Come here. I need to hold you." Keres drew her back to his chest, loving how she wiggled against him slightly to get comfortable before softening.

"Will you teach me how to be as ferocious as you?" she whispered.

"No."

"No?" She twisted to face him.

"I will teach you to defend yourself," he promised.

Rimi tilted her head as she considered his statement. "Okay. That's good."

He helped her recline once again. The sounds next door vanished quickly. Keres reached for a soft cloth on the edge of the tub. After dipping it into the water, he added a few drops of a gentle soap and stroked the washcloth over her shoulder and down Rimi's arm. She sighed with pleasure and tilted her head, silently inviting him to continue.

With pleasure, he continued to wash his mate. "Close your eyes, Snowflake. Let me wash your face."

"Can you wash my hair? It's dirty."

"Of course. I'll get that when I'm finished with your bath."

Keres loved Rimi's curves. His cock reacted to her closeness and the feel of her skin under his fingertips. Ignoring his desires, Keres focused on his mate. They would have years together to explore each other sexually. He could wait until she had recovered from the long journey.

"Sit up, Little one. Let me wash your back," he requested.

Rimi stiffened against him, launching herself away from him. "Little? Are you making fun of my size?"

Keres sat up and lifted her easily from the water before turning Rimi to face him. "No, Mate. I love everything about you." He drew her rigid body forward until she brushed against the proof of his desire. "There is no part of you I don't desire."

She stopped struggling. "Then why did you call me Little?"

"Daddies often refer to their matches as being Little. It's a term of endearment."

"Oh!"

"Rimi, can you think of one time since I found you that I've ever said anything negative about you or your enchanting form?"

"Um, no?"

"Definitely not. Why do you assume I would judge you harshly?"

"I don't want to tell you. You'll get mad."

"Perhaps." He didn't deny that possibility.

"About thirty years ago, I was captured by a sapphire dragon. He wasn't nice about my human form."

"What did he say?" Keres could hear the anger behind his words and tried to control his expression.

"That even rare creatures needed to make an effort to be attractive. And how cursed he was to find the only fat female dragon in the world."

Keres turned his head as literal steam exploded from his nostrils. It took him a full minute to get himself under control. "Tell me that bastard is dead."

"I think so. I was so mad, I kicked him in the nuts. When he leaned forward to cup himself, I let the blade go, and it chopped his head in half. I didn't wait to make sure he was completely gone. I got out of there."

"Fuck!" Keres pulled her close to him, squeezing her tightly. He detested his own species. How could anyone treat a precious creature so poorly? Deep down inside, he knew. That dragon had been further gone than he had been. Only someone who'd completely lost their mind could behave like that. "I'm so sorry, Rimi. I'm also very proud of you."

"I won't kick you in the balls," she promised.

Controlling his amusement at that vow, he watched her face as he said, "Thank you, Little One."

"You're welcome, D—Daddy."

That earned her a sizzling kiss. With immense effort, Keres dragged himself away from her alluring body. "You're going to call me that again when you're recovered and I can reward you," he told her.

She nodded and smiled. "I can't wait."

The minx challenged his self-control through the rest of her bath, shampoo, and snack. Keres loved every minute. He took a second to celebrate finding Rimi. Keres had never considered the possibility of having a female dragon as his mate. Now, he couldn't imagine his life without her.

Chapter 6

Opening her eyes in the stunning lilac room, Rimi lay perfectly still so she didn't interrupt her mate's sleep. She rotated her gaze from side to side, reassuring herself that she hadn't dreamed this. What an incredible change from a damp, dark cave where she worried every moment of every day that a male would arrive to claim her. Now stretched out on a fluffy mattress that cushioned every part of her body, Rimi tried to take it all in.

The drop-dead handsome shifter next to her rolled closer to press a kiss to her cheek. "It's still early, Mate. Do you want to go back to sleep?"

"I didn't mean to wake you," she apologized.

"You didn't." He kissed her softly before adding, "Welcome home."

"I hoped I hadn't dreamed all this."

"No, Snowflake. You're safe here. Well, at least from everyone other than me." He pulled her against him and kissed a line down her sensitive throat before pausing to ask, "Do you need to potty?"

Freezing, she considered his question before nodding.

"Thank you for telling me the truth." Keres rolled out of bed, taking her with him.

When he carried her to the door of the separate toilet room, Rimi reminded him, "I *can* walk."

"I enjoy holding you close. Now, go. I'll stay here today."

Rimi dashed into the small space and quickly sat down. She hoped he couldn't hear her tinkle. After she lived alone for so many years, doing things together with him seemed so alien.

Wait! What had he meant when he'd said, "I'll stay here today." Was he going to be somewhere else tomorrow? He didn't mean he would come in here when she peed? She finished and quickly opened the door to see if she could tell from his face.

"Yes. Doors will not separate us, mate. Let's wash your hands and then I have plans for you."

Taking advantage of flowing clean water, Rimi washed her face and her hands and took a drink. Wondering what his plans were, she set the small towel he'd handed her on the vanity and turned to face him.

"What's up?" she asked, studying his face.

"That's an excellent question," he answered with an amused expression on his face.

She glared at him. "Keres, stop playing games with me."

"Oh, I plan to play with you," he told her, stalking forward to hug her close. He lifted her feet from the ground and carried her back to the bed. He turned and fell backward onto the mattress, holding her tightly against him.

His hands caressed the length of her spine and over the full curve of her bottom. "I'm going to enjoy spanking this bottom."

An unexpected thrill went through her. Surely, he didn't mean what she thought he meant. Her gaze locked with his. "That's not going to happen."

"Oh, it will. I promise you'll both love and hate it."

Rimi pushed against his shoulders to sit up. She needed

some distance away from his hard deliciousness to think clearly. "Oh!" She figured out what he meant by "up" as his hard shaft slid across her lower lips.

Instantly, she tried to rise, but Keres held her in place with a firm grip around her hips. He gently shifted her back and forth across him. That brushing caress against her most intimate place made her gasp. Her juices welled from her, making the movement easier and parting her lower lips to allow him to move closer.

As she tried to conceal her arousal, Keres shared his with her, allowing her to experience the scorching desire and need inside him. She gasped as the flood of sensations scorched her mind. She stared at him in amazement before slamming her mouth onto his.

Kissing him with every bit of longing inside her, Rimi reveled in his reaction. His fingers bit into her hips as he struggled for control. She had tempted the beast inside him and now welcomed the consequences. She whispered against his lips, "You can't hurt me. Dragon, remember?"

His eyes flashed black before morphing into purple. They seemed to burn into hers. "I worship you, mate," he told her, his voice gravelly with need.

She pressed her hands to his chest and pushed herself up to sit straddling his hips. Holding his gaze, she rocked herself on his thick shaft. Rimi's breath caught in her throat as he sent shivers of sensations through her. He seemed to have memorized her most sensitive spots and targeted them with skill.

Keres lifted his hands to stroke up her torso. His rough skin caressed her curves, erasing any shame that jerk's statement had left with her. She could sense how much he appreciated her body—how tempting he found her.

She reached forward to explore the grooves in his muscular torso. He put the models she'd seen in discarded fashion and celebrity magazines to shame. When her hands roamed too close to his cock, Keres trapped her hand.

"I will welcome your caresses later, Mate."

She nodded and leaned back slightly to rub her hands over his thick thighs. Rimi knew she could get in trouble here, too, but it would be harder for him to stop her. She discovered the idea of tempting him appealed to her—tremendously.

His pelvis under her tilted slightly as Keres rolled up to sit. Their gazes met, and he gave her the "I know what you're doing" look. She rubbed the inside of his thigh and leaned forward to kiss that stern tilt to his mouth away. He nipped her bottom lip, sending a zing through her. Her heartrate jumped.

"You like a bit of pain," he observed.

Rimi shook her head desperately to refute that statement, but could tell he didn't believe her. To her astonishment, she was happy he didn't.

"Damn, I need to be inside you, Mate." He lifted her to her knees with one powerful hand at her waist. With the other, he caressed her intimately. "You are so wet. Are you ready for me?"

She gasped as his fingers slid into her depths. He held her steady as the sensations made her slightly wobbly.

"You're so hot. I can't wait to fill you."

"Please," she moaned. His fingers felt good, but she needed more.

Keres did not make her wait. Sliding his fingers free of her, he spread her slick juices over the head of his cock. The sight made her hum with excitement.

Aligning their bodies, he drew her downward as he filled her. He paused from time to time to allow her to relax before continuing inward. The pressure was intense as his thick shaft stretched her tight passage. Rimi dropped her head back, concentrating on the sensations.

She felt his hot breath on her neck a second before she felt his lips at the curve of her shoulder. His mouth opened, and he sucked lightly at her flesh before he nipped at her. That small bit of pain distracted her, and Keres thrust forward to slide into place.

Panting, Rimi's fingers tightened on his shoulders. She could feel what he did. The slick warmth of her pussy squeezed him tightly. Unable to resist, she tensed her internal muscles around him as she tilted her head to face him. His cock jerked inside her.

"You are temptation incarnate, Mate. Now you have to move." Keres guided her motions as she rose and lowered herself. He adjusted his movements until he found the angle that made her moan in delight.

"There. Please, there," she begged.

The sensations whirled around her as their skin glistened from the heat building between them. Rimi lost track of what she felt, and which sensations came from Keres. Without warning, pleasure exploded inside her. She screamed into the vast room before slapping a hand over her mouth to muffle the sound.

Keres pulled it away and pressed a kiss to her palm. "I want to hear all your sounds, Snowflake."

Building on her climax, Keres drove her to higher levels of excitement. By her third climax, the world around Rimi didn't exist. Only Keres mattered.

"One more, Mate. I need to feel you orgasm again."

"Keres, I don't think I can," she whispered.

"You can. I'll help you."

Keres hugged her torso tight against his as he changed their position. He shifted to kneeling before lowering Rimi's shoulders to the bed. He supported her pelvis with her body reclined at an angle. Keres thrust fully into her body, sinking a last few fractions of an inch deeper into her. Her hands tightened on his shoulders as he tapped the mouth of her womb.

As she recovered, Keres pulled out and thrust firmly back in. Increasing his speed, he built her arousal once again. When she hovered on the brink of coming again, he ground the root of his cock against her clit. That last caress was all she needed.

Keres pressed deep and exploded against the mouth of her womb. His hot juices splashed against her, filling her with his essence. Wrapping her legs around him instinctively, she held him deep inside her. He drooped over her, supporting his weight as they recovered.

She opened her eyes when he leaned forward to press his nose against her skin. "What's wrong?"

"Your scent just changed. You normally smell like jasmine. My nose thinks you have a hint of vanilla blended in with yours now."

"How could my scent change from within?" she asked, drawing the words out as she thought. She inhaled deeply. "I smell it, too."

Keres sniffed her shoulder. "I can smell it here, but it intensifies as I move lower on your body." He hovered over her stomach before going lower.

"Don't tell me my pussy smell like vanilla," she threatened.

"It does, but the strongest scent is here." He rubbed his powerful hand over her lower abdomen softly. "I think you're pregnant."

Her hand covered his. Focusing on that area, she sensed a new life inside her—a flutter of cells dividing and multiplying. She looked up at him in shock. How was this happening? "I can feel it, Keres. The baby."

Keres hauled her off the mattress to hug her tightly. His whoops of joy rattled the windows as he celebrated. He kissed her gently. "I'm going to wrap you in cotton, Snowflake. From losing my mind to finding the most alluring mate ever who happens to be a dragon and then creating a hatchling, you have turned my life upside down in an incredible way. Thank you, Mate"

She forced herself to smile at him as worries filled her mind. Was this a good thing or something tragic?

Chapter 7

Rimi bounced in place as the large bronze dragon circled and landed. Accompanying him was a blue dragon who carried a slight woman on his back. Keres had explained to her that Oldrik and Ardon shared a mate.

"Oldrik!" She raced forward to greet her brother and meet those special to him. His dragon was magnificent. So much different from the dragon he'd turned into the first time.

In a flash, he shifted and ran forward. To her dismay, he stopped a few feet short of her and held out a warning hand. "I would love to hug you, sister, but I do not wish to cause you pain."

"Pain? Why would you hurt me?" Rimi asked, completely confused by his actions.

Keres reassured her, "Rimi, I should have explained. A new mate bond protects the couple by discouraging contact with others. It also causes pain when you range too far from your shifter."

"Were you struck with pain when you ran to greet me?" Oldrik asked.

"No. I didn't feel anything but excitement to meet you," Rimi told him, bewildered.

"Perhaps because you're a dragon, things are different for you. Let's try this." Oldrik stepped forward to hug Rimi and stopped in his tracks when a vicious, low growl rumbled from Keres's throat.

Laughing, Oldrik commented, "Looks like things are different for you, Rimi, but Keres needs you to stay away from me for a while."

"Or forever," Keres suggested.

Rimi shook her head and turned back to her brother. "My goodness, you have grown up. Your dragon is huge!"

"And you are as lovely as always. Have you been okay? I didn't want to leave you alone."

"You had to, Oldrik. You would have endangered me more if you'd stayed with me. One dragon might succeed at hiding their presence. Two would never have survived. Besides, you had a horde and mates waiting for you." Rimi honestly didn't harbor any resentment toward her twin. The ways of their species weren't his responsibility.

"Thank you, Rimi. I'm glad fate has brought us together again."

Oldrik sniffed the air around her. His gaze locked with hers. Her twin had always been perceptive. *Say nothing, please.*

He nodded subtly. "Let me introduce you to my mate and my bonus." Oldrik turned to smile at the willowy blonde who approached. He held out his hand and tugged her close.

Rimi could feel love arching between the couple as well as the other shifter who approached. Keres had referred to them as a triad.

"This is Skye and Ardon."

"Hi. It's great to meet you both." To her dismay, Rimi heard her voice tremble. Standing out in the open and meeting people scared her. She'd hidden for too many years away from everyone. Suddenly, this was too much for her. Keres wrapped a protective arm around her waist. She knew he would save her from any threat.

"We will go inside," Skye announced and stepped away from Oldrik to walk next to Rimi.

Giving Skye a glance of bone-deep gratitude, Rimi tried to walk at a normal pace when she really wanted to flee. Why had she dashed so far away from the house to meet Oldrik?

"We can run if you'd like," Skye told her.

"I need to learn that I'm safe now. I'm sorry. You may not—not know what's—what's wrong with me," Rimi stammered.

"Everyone has something wrong with them," Skye reassured her simply, and then gave her an assessing look. *Can you hear me?*

Yes. You are easy to understand. How can you talk to someone other than your mate?

Keres was the first dragon I met. He could hear me, too.

I think she loves dragons so much, she can talk to everyone, Keres stated, obviously fond of the petite mate.

Rimi didn't like that.

It's easier for me to talk through thoughts. Keres was the first person to answer me. Skye explained. *I drew a picture of him. He put it up somewhere.*

It is in my office. Let's go there to talk and Rimi can see it.

Deciding to keep an eye on this other mate in case she had designs on Keres, too, Rimi followed her mate into his office. Keres waved his guests into the comfortable seating area by the windows. Oldrik and Ardon selected a wide sofa and Skye climbed on Oldrik's lap to snuggle against his chest. The move was natural and practiced. Watching them together, Rimi's suspicions of Skye being out to steal her mate evaporated.

Keres sat in an oversized armchair and scooped Rimi onto

his lap. Still rattled by the outside incident, she appreciated sitting in the circle of his powerful arms. Her mate's closeness soothed and reassured her. Skye must feel the same way.

"Did you sense you were mates instantly?" Ardon asked.

"She tried to chop my head off," Keres said easily. "Then she dropped an entire mountain of rocks on top of me."

"I did not!" Rimi said, shaking her finger at him. When he quirked an eyebrow at her, she admitted, "Okay, I released that blade to protect myself."

Good for you, Skye cheered her on.

"Thank you. And the rocks came from him burying us alive to keep two marauding dragons out of the cave," Rimi explained.

"And it collapsed as you dug your way out?" Ardon guessed.

"Exactly," Rimi answered before muttering, "I dropped rocks on your head."

"A slight exaggeration, perhaps," Keres admitted. "We both felt the bombshell when we touched."

Did I see you both have mate marks? Skye asked, holding up her hand to display the dragon on her skin.

"We do. Is that unusual?" Rimi asked.

"I've never seen a mate mark on a dragon. Only on a human," Oldrik told her. "Perhaps because you're both dragons?"

"Who knows?" Keres said, shrugging. He'd already told Rimi he didn't care whether they were the only mated dragons in the world. She loved that he simply cared about her.

You love him.

Rimi's gaze ricocheted from Skye to Keres, who described his journey to the other shifters.

They can't hear me. Only you, Skye reassured her. *I'm sorry. I didn't mean to scare you.*

I haven't told him yet.
Do you think your feelings will change?
No. Never.

Skye beamed at her. *I'm glad Keres found you, Rimi. He needed love.*

So did I, Rimi admitted.

My picture of Keres is on the wall behind Keres's desk.

Rimi slid off Keres's lap and walked closer. It was an astonishing piece of art. Her mate was majestic in his powerful dragon form, yet Skye had woven a sad note skillfully into the design. She had realized Keres's time was limited as she crafted the portrait. Tears gathered in Rimi's eyes.

Would you let me draw you together in dragon form to replace that one? He's not alone anymore.

Turning to meet Skye's gaze, Rimi nodded. *I would like that. It may take me a while to become comfortable outside,* Rimi warned.

I bet Keres can empty a ballroom or something.

I bet you're right.

In unison, the two women turned to stare at the dragons lounging together. Ardon noticed them watching.

"Do I need to get a sketchpad from home?" he asked.

Yes, please. Oldrik and Keres can clear out a room while you're gone, Skye announced.

"Anyone want to bet he won't get back until we've moved a thousand pieces of furniture?" Oldrik joked.

"Oh, I'll make sure that happens," Ardon said and chuckled as he walked to the door.

Rimi wrapped her arms around herself as she looked between those filling Keres's office. She was welcome here. Keres stood and hugged her tightly.

"Come, Snowflake. Skye will probably like the library. It is very spacious without the furniture," he suggested.

Do you have a cave? Maybe one with glowing light?

Keres met her gaze and smiled. *I think I have exactly what you're imagining, Skye.*

Chapter 8

Rimi wondered what the drawing would look like when Skye finished. From Oldrik and Ardon's expressions as they peeked from time to time, it had to be incredible. The lighting in the cave changed her scales from sparkling white crystal in the sunlight to a rosy hue. Keres was magnificent, of course. Seeing him in dragon form made Rimi appreciate his masculine attributes. He was hot.

Thank you, Snowflake. I enjoy making you melt.

Keres! Shhh! Rimi hoped the others hadn't overheard that conversation.

Relax, Mate. I would never share our intimacies with anyone. Are you okay? Skye will draw for hours if we permit it. Would you like her to continue on another day?

Suddenly, she needed to move. *Please.*

Keres immediately broadcast to everyone. *Skye, my mate is tiring. We will have to pose for you again on a different day.*

I've got enough to finish this on my own, Skye reported. *Sorry, I was having too much fun to stop.*

Amused by her new friend's honesty, Rimi didn't blame her

at all for not saying anything. She rose to her feet and stretched her tight muscles. Who knew that staying still would take so much energy?

The three male shifters shook their heads. Rimi could sense their affection toward Skye. Keres's affection for her differed from those of her loving mates, of course, but Rimi could tell her mate cared about Skye.

You are much more important to me than Skye, Snowflake, Keres reassured her.

I know. I like that you have friends who you care about and who look out for you.

You are now part of the group, Rimi, Keres confidently told her.

Skye closed her sketchpad, concealing her efforts. She walked to stand in front of Rimi. *Thank you. I will show you the final image when it's done, if that's okay?*

Of course, Skye. I can't wait to see what you create.

Her brother guided Skye to a safe location before Rimi and Keres shifted into human form. The safeguarding action reminded Rimi of their time as kids together. Of course, they'd played and had fun together, but Oldrik had focused on protecting her. When he had to leave, Rimi had limited their communication. Her place in the dragon world was not his fault or responsibility. Her love for her brother had forced her to set him free. Rimi loved seeing him happy today.

Keres wrapped an arm around her waist and pulled her close. Meeting his eyes, Rimi knew he had followed her thoughts.

"You are very strong, Snowflake," he complimented her.

"Me? No way."

"You aren't seeing it from my perspective, Little one."

A sudden wave of nausea overtook her. Rimi clapped her hand over her mouth and ran for the cave entrance. Keres shouted her name, but she didn't stop. Once outside, she lost the battle and vomited.

"Let me help you," Keres said gently as he gathered her hair in his hands.

The buzz in her head told her he communicated with their guests, but she felt too horrible to pay attention. When her stomach was empty, Keres pulled off his shirt to wipe her mouth and hands clean. He lifted her into his arms.

"Poor baby." He comforted her and carried her into the mansion and to their bedroom. In the attached bathroom, he stripped off her soiled clothes as he shushed her apologies. "You're allowed to be sick, Little girl. Let Daddy take care of you."

"Daddy, I feel awful."

"I'm sorry, Rimi. Let's see if I can make you more comfortable." He washed her face and hands before gently easing one of his giant T-shirts over her head. "Would you like to stretch out for a while?"

She started to nod, but stopped when the motion reignited her nausea. Rimi whispered, "yes," instead.

In a short while, Keres tucked her in bed. Rimi tried to find a comfortable position, but was too restless to stay still. Keres brushed her hair out of her face and kissed her cheek.

"Let's try this, Mate." He placed a cool washcloth on her forehead, and the tension eased. "Better?"

"Mmmhmmm."

"I have a present for you, Little girl. He'll scare the sick away so you can rest."

Rimi heard a rustle and opened her eyes to see the black velvety material in front of her. She reached out to stroke it. "Soft," she whispered and then hesitated before asking, "A present for me?"

"Yes, Snowflake. The black dragon is all yours. You'll have to come up with a name."

She tugged the stuffie from his hand and pulled it close, hugging it to her chest. "He'll tell me his name when he's ready. Dragons are bossy sometimes."

"They are indeed. Close your eyes, Rimi. See if you can rest."

In a few minutes, her breath smoothed.

🐲🐲🐲

"Daddy?" Rimi's whisper alerted Keres.

"Hi, Snowflake. Do you feel better?"

"We're hungry."

"We're?" Keres questioned.

"Yes. Rumble and me. We're hungry." She shook the black dragon stuffie at him.

"Rumble? He told you his name?"

"Yes, Daddy, and he's starving."

"I'm sensing urgency here, Snowflake. Let's go to the kitchen and see what we can find that Rumble wants to eat."

He helped her out of bed. Did her stomach seem more rounded than usual? It must be his oversized T-shirt. "Let's find something for you to use as a robe."

"I'll put on my clothes," she blurted.

"Are you comfortable in my T-shirt?"

"Yes, but your staff..."

"They will smile at you and be glad you're here. Believe me, everyone working on my estate doesn't care what you are wearing."

Keres zipped into his closet and returned with a soft cotton robe he'd forgotten he even had. He helped Rimi into it and drew the belt around her waist. His hands stilled on her much rounder tummy.

"Food, Keres. I need to eat," she said urgently.

"Should we fly?" he asked.

Rimi nodded. "Rumble will stay here. Can we go now?"

Keres rushed her through the mansion and out to the front lawn. He shifted as soon as she triggered her change and powered into the air to protect her. When she joined him, Keres guided her to his livestock fields.

He drove the plumpest beasts toward his mate one at a time until she failed to attack. Flying to that side of the field, he devoured the last cow for her. Keres landed next to her and rubbed his snout across the crystal dragon's.

Rimi? How are you?

Better. I've never felt like that. My body demanded food.

It's the hatchling. He needs nourishment to grow, Keres suggested.

She nodded and yawned. *I'm exhausted again.*

Home and sleep, Mate.

For three days, Keres helped Rimi shift from sleep to feasting. Each time she woke up, her belly had grown. Her current waddle enchanted him. She couldn't get any cuter.

"Keres, I need to go somewhere safe. Can you take me back to the cave where we posed for Skye?"

"Of course."

Keres had learned over the last hours not to argue, but to help Rimi with whatever she needed. He supported her as they made their way to the cave entrance. Off balance from her enormous belly, Rimi moved slowly. Halfway there, she bent over to wrap her arms around her stomach. Her cry of pain sliced through Keres.

"Rimi! What can I do?"

"Get me to the cave, Keres. Now!"

Lifting her into his arms, Keres sped for the entrance and eased his precious cargo through the slim opening. He breathed a sigh of relief as they emerged into the enormous cavern. When he lowered Rimi's feet toward the ground, she pointed to the spot where she had lain for Skye's picture. "There."

He carried her to that spot. Rimi sank to the ground, clutching her belly. Sitting behind her, he rubbed her back, trying desperately to help. He reached out to her mentally and staggered under the pain that ricocheted inside her mind. Quickly, he pulled as much agony into his mind as he could. Her sigh of relief told Keres to continue.

"I need to undress, Keres," she whispered.

Immediately, he freed her of unneeded clothing. Her scream quickened his efforts. Wrapping his arms around her straining body, Keres supported her weight.

"I've got you, Snowflake."

"You're never touching me again," she groaned.

Keres grinned from behind her. That prediction wouldn't come true. "Let's worry about our future sex life later, hmmm?"

"Never," she spat out like a curse before screaming again. "Something's happening, Keres. Help me shift." Acting instinctively, Rimi listened to her dragon's demands. Keres was by her side the whole way. His strength supported her from behind as she allowed nature to take over. Keres filled her mind with encouragement to bolster her energy and surround her with positive thoughts as he continued to drain the pain through their mental connection. After an hour of struggle, her brilliant dragon form curled around a sparkling crystal egg. Keres's darkness formed a protective barrier to any threat.

Keres inched his beast's head forward to sniff at the gorgeous shell and about lost half his snout. His mate was a bit protective. He would keep his distance until she would allow him to check out their offspring.

Retreating, Keres took a protective stance over his mate. He would give his life to keep them safe. A wave of love wafted his way from Rimi. She was counting on him.

Chapter 9

Rimi? What is happening?

At the sound of her twin's voice resounding inside her mind, Rimi blinked her eyes open and spotted Keres standing guard over her. Instantly, his gaze met hers. She nodded that she and the hatchling were okay.

Oldrik. I am fine. Keres is here with me.

We all felt a wave of distress. What is going on? Did Keres attack you?

A growl of anger resounded around the cave. Rimi sent reassurance to her bristling mate.

No, Oldrik. Keres would end himself before hurting me or the hatchling.

The hatchling? Astonishment echoed in his voice. *What hatchling?*

The one I'm currently wrapped around to keep it warm.

She felt his attention shift slightly and then heard Oldrik say to Skye, *You knew? Let me see your picture.*

What's in Skye's drawing, Oldrik? Rimi asked.

It's the pose from the cave. With an addition. There's a sparkling white egg next to you, Oldrik reported.

79

I wish Skye had clued me in, Rimi said with a mental chuckle.

You're okay?

I'm really good, Oldrik. I have no clue what I'm doing, but the hatchling seems to let me know what it needs.

It? Can you tell if it's a male? Oldrik asked.

It hasn't told me, Oldrik. Do I sense Ardon close by?

He is on the first watch outside the cave. Ask for whatever your family needs, Rimi. The horde is protecting you.

Keres joined the conversation, including all the members of the horde. *Thank you. Remain outside. My dragon is not tolerant at the present. Seeing our mate in pain was torture.*

It wasn't too much fun on this side, either, Rimi chimed in.

We will make sure no one disturbs you, Drake promised.

Rimi met Keres's gaze to reassure him before dropping her head back to the ground to rest. Her family was protected.

One week later, Keres emerged into the sunlight. The brightness made him blink as his eyes adjusted. Spotting three dragons circling above them and two standing guard a short distance away, he drew Rimi through the opening. The hatchling filled her arms to almost overflowing. Its adorable head rested on her shoulder.

Aahs filled the air as the mates got their first glimpse of the baby. Obviously warned by their dragons, Skye, Lalani, Brooks, Ciel, and Aurora stood away from the opening. Each held binoculars to their eyes so they could get a close view of the hatchling.

"So cute!" Aurora called, and the others chimed in with their good wishes.

The hatchling didn't rouse. Having recently shared the

dragon-family-sized feast delivered earlier by Keres's staff, the small dragon had a full belly and snoozed deeply. As if on cue, the beast shifted into human form in Rimi's arms, drawing more admiration from the crowd before reverting back to his dragon.

Rimi glanced at Keres and nodded, as if urging him to say something.

"Thank you all for the many hours of vigilance you have given our offspring. We would like you to meet Slate. He is a perfect combination of my mate and I," Keres announced.

"It's a boy," Oldrik announced with relief.

"We would have welcomed a girl with equal excitement, but yes, Slate is male. Be warned, he has an evil streak from his sire and wisdom from his mother," Keres shared.

"So, he's wickedly smart? That's not a good combination," Drake said with a chuckle.

"Of course it is," Aurora corrected him with a glare.

"We will take our son into our mansion now that he can change into human form," Keres shared. "He is able to defend himself now."

"He's still a baby," Rimi said quickly.

The dragon shifters all looked at her indulgently. Dragons grew quickly. For their survival, they were only vulnerable for a short time. Once they could shift, they doubled or tripled in size each day until they reached full size. Slate's tail extended a few more inches to drag on the floor before their eyes. Rimi wouldn't be able to carry him after today.

"He needs to eat, Rimi. I will take him to the near field. Would you like to offer our guests refreshments?"

Rimi forced herself to set Slate down on the grass. She had loved bonding with the small creature she and Keres had created together. Letting him become independent was heart-wrenching.

"Rimi, I'm so glad to spend time with you," Lalani said, slipping her hand around Rimi's arm and squeezing it slightly.

"I've never been inside Keres' house. Is it completely black inside?" Brooks asked.

"Our room is lilac colored. I love it. Slate's room is gray. I hope he will like it," Rimi said, worried.

"Of course he will. Come, show it to us," Ciel requested.

"Maybe after he sees it first?" Rimi suggested. It didn't seem right to share her offspring's room with others before he had the opportunity to claim it. Dragons were funny about their space.

Ciel laughed at herself. "What a silly suggestion! I didn't think."

"You could show them my picture of you," Skye suggested, smoothly filling the awkwardness. Rimi smiled at her in relief.

"Of course. It's in Keres's office."

Glad to have a distraction from the worry filling her mind, Rimi led everyone into the mansion to her mate's space. There, on the wall behind his desk, hung the now colorful painting Skye had created. Everyone gathered around to see how the talented artist had created the scene before Rimi and Keres had shared the news of their hatchling.

"You told your brother and his mates about the baby first," Brooks said with a nod of approval.

"No. We didn't tell anyone. Oldrik knew from my scent," Rimi said. "Skye must have guessed?"

"How did you sense Rimi would have a baby?" Aurora asked, turning toward Skye.

"I could hear him."

"You knew he was a male?" Rimi asked in complete disbelief.

"Yes. Sorry, I knew first. I didn't tell anyone. Not even Oldrik and Ardon," Skye reported.

"I love this picture, Skye. Now I have to ask—how did you know to ask Keres if he had a cave with good lighting?"

"The question popped into my brain. I don't know where it came from. Honestly," Skye assured her.

"It's okay, Skye. I'm not upset. This is astonishing. I love this picture," Rimi assured her.

"It's Slate's first baby picture," Lalani pointed out.

"His only," Rimi said with a smile. Her hatchling wasn't a baby anymore. Slate would be a full dragon in days.

"Miss Rimi, I have set up refreshments for your guests in the living room."

"Thank you, Russell," Rimi said with a smile to Keres's butler. His staff would always have a special place in her heart. They had shown him loyalty, even when his growing madness endangered their lives.

"My pleasure. If you will follow me," Russell said and led the way to the room where comfortable chairs beckoned everyone to relax.

A few minutes later, the mates sat with plates filled with delicacies from the kitchen. Russell delivered a plate for her with generous samples of everything. After struggling to find food repeatedly throughout her life, Rimi still battled an urge to claim everything for herself. It was easier to have someone to serve her. Besides, she had no idea what anything was.

Thankfully, no one said anything about her not visiting the buffet. She selected a cheese cube and popped it into her mouth. *Yum!* Russell had done it again, choosing items she would love.

"Could you all tell me about yourselves?" Rimi asked. "I'd like to get to learn more about each of you."

"Of course. Brooks?" Aurora prompted.

"They always make me go first," Brooks said with a charming grin. "I'm Rogan's mate. He's the red dragon. I met Skye on her way back to Wyvern along with another guy I happened to run into from our town. We stuck together for the trip home. I hung around for a while and met Rogan."

"You mean three of you from Wyvern ran into each other on the way back here? The odds of that must be astronomical," Rimi marveled. Just watching the number of humans wandering around, going in all directions, had amazed her.

"I'm sure fate had a hand in putting us together," Brooks suggested and glanced at Skye, who nodded her agreement.

"I'll go next. I'm Aurora. Believe it or not, I ran into Drake at the funeral of his previous mate. That was disconcerting, to say the least."

"Drake's the gold dragon, right?" Rimi asked.

"Yes. The hunkiest one," Aurora said.

An uproar followed as the mates debated that bold statement. Rimi could tell they all enjoyed getting together from the teasing and chatter. She hoped she could be part of the group, even though she was so different from them.

After hearing Lalani's story of being adopted and growing up elsewhere, Ciel introduced herself as the silver dragon's mate. "The funniest thing is that we all have childhood dragon stuffies. I think they all came from the same store in the old section of town."

"Keres gave me one," Rimi blurted, not realizing what she'd just revealed.

"You're Little?" Lalani asked before shaking her head and apologizing, "I'm sorry. I shouldn't have asked."

Several of the mates had rosy cheeks now, and Ciel and

Brooks avoided Rimi's eyes. "It's okay. You can ask me anything. If I don't know or don't want to answer, I'll tell you. I'll be honest, I'd never heard of that term before meeting Keres."

"He's talked to you about it?" Aurora asked.

"Yes, when he gave me Rumble. That's my dragon."

"I love that name. Mine is Silly. He's a silver dragon," Ciel shared.

"It turns out we all have a lot in common. That's probably the fated mate thing," Brooks pointed out. "Perhaps there's a personality component to all of us, in addition to our family roots."

"Did you ever think you'd be a dragon's mate?" Lalani asked.

"No. I knew a dragon would capture me at some point. My mother didn't share any details about how Oldrik and I were conceived. My impression was that her survival after our hatching was unusual," Rimi told them.

"Female dragons do not have easy lives. You'd think the other dragons would treat them like queens," Brooks stated fiercely. Rimi could tell he was ashamed of his sex.

An image of her sitting on a gold throne heavily adorned with jewels popped into her head, and she chuckled. Noting their quizzical looks, she said, "Sorry, I pictured myself like a queen bee there for a moment in all my regalia."

"I want to see that. We need to have another tiara party," Aurora suggested, earning a groan from Brooks. "You can wear your ruby crown, Brooks. That will be extremely manly."

"Deal," he agreed. "Has Keres shown you his hoard?"

"No," Rimi said, shrugging. "Does he have one?"

"Oh, yeah. Keres has one," Ciel laughed. "All the dragons do. Hey, you should have one, too. Keres should create a space for your own lair."

Rimi shook her head. "I'm sure a female doesn't get a treasure spot."

"Who says? There aren't any others to ask," Skye pointed out. Her voice made everyone turn. Skye didn't speak often. When she did, they listened.

As if on cue, the shifters walked in. All the mates turned in unison to look at them. Keres arched an eyebrow at their attention.

"Why do I think we got here at the wrong time?"

"We were just discussing tiaras and the fact that Rimi doesn't have one. And that led to us asking if she had her own hoard. Don't all dragons have a hoard?" Ciel asked in a sugary, innocent tone that made Argenis shake his head.

The other dragon shifters stepped away from Keres in a deliberate attempt to distance themselves with a blended "Ooh!" of sympathy.

"Keres, it's not important," Rimi rushed to assure him.

"It is, Snowflake. We will work on remedying that when we finish our visit with our guests," Keres assured her, seeming completely unfazed by the attention.

"Mommy?" Slate called her name to get Rimi's attention before climbing up on her lap. Already, he was almost too big.

"You're getting so big. How many cows did you eat?" Rimi asked, groaning under his weight dramatically to entertain the young dragon.

"Two!" he announced proudly.

"Two whole cows?" Rimi asked in amazement.

"Well, Daddy helped with the last one," Slate admitted.

Keres rubbed his flat stomach. "It's a tough job being a parent" he whined, making everyone laugh.

When the shifters had settled with their mates, Keres asked, "Catch us up. Is there any news about the powder attacks?"

"It's been quiet since the two guys in Rogan's barn alerted us about the shipment coming in. We caught that before it hit the border. When you're ready to join the patrols again, message us," Drake told him.

"More will come," Argenis predicted. "I think we're dealing with some kind of fanatic. It has to be one person pulling the strings. Who knows what his motivation is, but he is definitely targeting dragons."

"All we can be is vigilant and make sure those in our inner circle are loyal," Drake suggested.

"The news of Slate's birth will spread," Keres commented warily.

"That will piss them off," Oldrik predicted.

"Count me in on patrols immediately," Keres added.

"Can I ask what the powder attacks are?" Rimi asked. She wanted to learn about anything they felt would affect Slate.

"Oh, you haven't heard?" Lalani asked.

"A faction of humans have discovered a powdery substance that is lethal to dragons and humans alike. They have orchestrated attacks against almost all the horde," Keres explained.

"Will they come after us?" Rimi asked, glancing deliberately at Slate.

"It is possible. Slate, do not go off on your own until we eliminate this threat," Keres instructed.

Limiting a young dragon's freedom was almost impossible. Hopefully, Slate would heed his sire's instructions.

"You can protect me, Slate, when Keres is on patrol."

"No way. I'm going with him."

Chapter 10

"What's a crystal dragon's superpower?" Skye broke the tension that followed Slate's declaration.

Pleased to have something else to focus on, Rimi turned to meet her gaze, sending this mental message, *Thank you, Skye.* Then to everyone, she asked, "Superpowers?"

"Some things have to be experienced," Keres said mysteriously as he waggled his eyebrows suggestively. Rimi's cheeks heated with embarrassment.

"Keres!" she said in exasperation.

"La, la, la, la, la! Things a twin does not need to hear," Oldrik commented, adding humor to the conversation.

"Speaking of hearing, that reminds me. Keres, do you have a map of Wyvern and the surrounding area? I had a report of loud music coming from a nearby city and I'm not sure where it is," Ardon said.

"Of course. Come with me. We'll figure it out," Keres said, leading the dragon shifters to his office.

Rimi sighed in relief as Slate slid from her lap to follow the dragons. She bounced her knees up and down, relaxing her muscles. "I think his time on my lap is over."

The mates laughed. Even in human form, dragon shifters weighed more than a normal individual. She suspected they'd all tried to move their mates and found them impossible to shift.

"Can you all tell me about Wyvern? How did the dragons get involved?"

"I think we were all clueless about dragons until all the tech died," Aurora told her. "At least I was."

Everyone nodded.

"Then the dragons were super involved in finding and returning everyone to Wyvern," Ciel told her. "We got used to seeing them in the sky and on the ground. It still fascinates me to see them shift. It feels like I miss a split second of something magical each time. Does it hurt to shift?"

Rimi nodded. "It can. If you're not in good health, it's a tremendous strain on both the dragon and the human part of you."

She took a deep breath and plunged in. "Can you tell me about Keres? He came to find me, thinking it was the end for him. Was he violent?"

"I think he scared everyone and saved all of us at some point," Brooks confessed. "Skye and he have the closest relationship between the horde and other dragons' mates. She could talk to him in dragon form."

"He's my favorite after my Daddies, of course," Skye told Rimi with a smile. "He needed to find you. That's all."

"I'm glad he did," Rimi said. It didn't bother her at all that Skye and Keres were close. She'd already figured that out. The bond between Skye and her mates was strong. As was hers with Keres. Jealousy toward the unique woman was impossible.

"We are, too," Lalani told her warmly.

Rimi relaxed more with each moment she spent with the mates. She'd never had friends, of course. All that hiding and people searching for her interfered with the possibility.

"Are you happy here, Rimi?" Skye asked.

"Yes. I'm safe and loved. That's a huge difference from my life before Keres found me."

"Do you think you'll have more children?" Brooks asked before holding up his hand to stop Rimi's answer. "I'm sorry. That was a stupid question and totally none of my business."

Tension suddenly filled the air. The mates weren't sure how she would react. Rimi laughed before admitting, "I don't know. There isn't birth control for dragons."

"Just flame Keres if he gets frisky," Ciel suggested.

Two long seconds passed as no one looked at each other. A snort escaped from Rimi as she tried to keep herself from laughing at the thought of being able to resist Keres's tempting ways. That wouldn't ever happen.

Immediately, everyone lost it. Lalani even spat a mouthful of water through the air as she tried to control herself. The staff came in to make sure everyone was okay before leaving, grinning themselves. Their mirth was infectious.

As if on cue, the shifters returned. Argenis scooped Ciel up in his arms and sat down with her on his lap. One by one, the dragons followed that pattern, confiscating a seat and cuddling their mates. Oldrik took the empty seat between Rimi and Skye, allowing Ardon to hold their mate.

"Rimi, do you have a nursery?" Aurora asked.

"She has not seen it yet," Keres shared as he easily lifted Rimi into his arms and sat down. "We've been a bit busy with Slate."

"Where is Slate?" Rimi asked, glancing around. Even though everyone else was seated on someone's lap, she felt slightly embarrassed.

Keres kissed her temple. "He went to his room. He's fine, Snowflake."

Rimi nodded and tried to relax. She replayed his earlier statement in her mind. "I have a... A nursery?"

"You do. Every mate needs a quiet space of their own. We will add whatever you like to the room. Books, puzzle, crafts."

"I love to read. I've found a few tattered books here and there. They were a wonderful escape."

"Then we will add books to your nursery," Keres assured her.

"We all like to read, too," Lalani blurted.

The reaction of all the mates made Rimi pause. Why had they all turned red? Maybe she needed to read these books as well. "Would you recommend some for me?"

"Of course," Ciel said and everyone giggled.

"Ciel is a writer," Aurora shared.

"I'd love to read something you created," Rimi said and scanned the group as their mates laughed again. And what was that expression on the dragon shifters' faces? Something was definitely up. She couldn't wait to read Ciel's stories and their other suggestions.

"Who would like to hunt with Slate next week?" Keres asked, changing the subject when the conversation lagged.

"Hunt? A baby can't hunt," Lalani cried out in concern.

"His baby stage ended the day after he was born," Khadar told her. "Dragons grow up fast. Count me in, Keres."

The others indicated they would join as well. It was an important step for the young dragon. Keres nodded his thanks to each member of his horde.

"Would the mates like to join Rimi for a luncheon? She would love to have company, I am sure," Keres added.

"Doesn't she go hunting?" Ciel asked.

"This is a male-only expedition." Keres laid down the law, ignoring the fumes of anger that rippled toward him from not only his dragon-shifter mate, but the other mates. His gaze met

Brooks's, and he quickly clarified, "Male dragon only, I should say."

"Of course," Brooks said after checking in with Rogan. "I would love to keep you company, Rimi. I will be here."

The other mates chimed in quickly. No one would make the mother stay by herself as her baby went out into the world for the first time. Even if that baby had sharp teeth, dangerous talons, and fiery breath.

🐉 🐉 🐉

"It's okay, Rimi. I will stay by Slate's side. He's already mastered flying and how to dispatch prey. This is simply the next step," Keres told her.

"It's a huge, bounding leap into adulthood, Keres!" She hugged Rumble to her chest and glanced toward the bedroom door. Slate had his own room in the next wing. He preferred to be away from his parents at night. Rimi knew he snuck out to explore. It wouldn't be too long before he left to find his own horde.

"Slate will be fine," Keres told her. "I wouldn't arrange this hunt if he wasn't. Trust me?"

"Of course, but couldn't I go, too?"

"No, Snowflake. No women allowed."

He wouldn't budge. Arrggh! This was so unfair. Before she could stop herself, Rimi picked up the closest object and threw it at Keres. The lamp shattered harmlessly against the bedroom door. Rimi raced around the bed to rearm herself with the other one. She didn't make it.

"You are acting very poorly, Mate. I think it's time you found out what happens to Little girls who throw things at their Daddies."

Keres stalked forward. Rimi drew the lamp back to toss it at him, but he was too fast. She struggled to hold on to the lamp, but her mate stripped it out of her hands with ease.

"Give me that."

"Your level of violence toward lighting is troubling, Snowflake. Especially since that no longer works," he said, grasping her wrist with his free hand as he casually set the lamp back on the nightstand.

"Let me go!" she demanded, twisting her arm in a vain attempt to free herself. He was too strong for her to get away.

"No. It's time for you to learn a lesson. There's only one Daddy in this relationship. And one naughty Little." Keres sat down on the bed and drew her between his legs.

"All spankings are applied to a naked bottom." He unfastened her jeans and pushed them over her hips.

Rimi considered kicking his shins, but reality dawned on her. He was too strong, even for her. She swallowed hard, trying not to react. Her body had other ideas. They hadn't been intimate since Slate had made his arrival. Simply being around Keres had an arousing effect on her—being half naked skyrocketed her response.

Rimi struggled to pull away from him, but Keres controlled her easily. He lifted her feet from the carpet and rotated her to stretch over his lap. His hand stroked over her naked bottom.

"My precious Little. Perhaps I've given you too much time to recover from Slate's birth. Let me remind you who is in charge."

Rearing her torso up at the first slap on her bottom, Rimi gasped at the sting. "That hurt!"

"Of course, it did."

Keres spanked her several times in succession before rubbing his palm over her skin. Before she could recover, he started again, raining swats over her tender flesh. A thought burst into her mind. *I'm a dragon!* She could partially shift to give herself protection from the stinging punishment.

"Not happening, Little girl," Keres growled as scales appeared on her bottom. He wrapped a hand around the back of her neck and asserted his dominance. Instantly, her dragon traits receded. "I could spank you in either form, Snowflake," he reminded her.

As the heat built on her skin, tears gathered in her eyes. She didn't want him to see her cry, but she couldn't fight his control over her. Rimi slumped over his legs, submitting to Keres fully.

"That's my good girl." Keres praised her and shifted his next slap.

Rimi inhaled sharply when his powerful hand landed between her legs. Her pussy throbbed, and she spread her legs wider, inviting his caresses again. "Please."

Keres repeated that erotic "punishment" three more times before returning to swat her bottom. Needing more, Rimi squirmed on his lap. Now the sting of her spanking blended with growing arousal.

When he lingered to play in the growing slickness, she begged once again, "Please, Keres."

"Daddy," he corrected her sternly.

"Please, Daddy," she recited.

"That's my good girl." Keres slid two fingers into her tight channel and brushed his thumb against her clit.

She climaxed immediately and screamed her pleasure into the room. Keres spanked her five more times as her body throbbed around his fingers, extending her pleasure and making her crave more.

"I need to be buried deep inside you, Snowflake," Keres growled. He stood and tossed her onto the mattress.

Holding her gaze, he licked her juices from his fingers. His eyes flashed purple, revealing his rampaging dragon. She shivered, wanting all of him—the beast and the man. With rough, hurried movements, he stripped off his clothing and crawled onto the bed.

His mouth captured hers, delivering a punishing kiss that demanded her full response. Keres ripped his mouth from hers and quickly tore off the rest of her clothing. His urgency pushed her arousal higher.

Rimi stroked her hands over his chest, caressing his hard muscles and basking in her mate's power. She hid a smile when he ripped her arms over her head and pinned her hands to the mattress. She loved that he battled for control.

He thrust forward, filling her completely. Rimi gasped as she wrapped her legs around his waist. She pressed kisses to his throat and across his jaw before whispering, "Move," into his ear.

His roar filled the space as he followed her request. His strokes pushed her arousal higher and higher until she could only think of him and the pleasure they created together. When the sensations inside reached a peak, her climax rocked her. Unable to hold back, she confessed her feelings. "I love you, Daddy!"

"I love you, too, Snowflake. Forever more."

She brushed the hair back from his face tenderly before whispering, "Forever more."

She would never get enough of him. Moving against his body, she urged him to find his pleasure. Keres rebuilt her arousal until they came together. Rimi didn't understand how fate had matched them together, but she would thank her lucky stars every day and every night.

Chapter 11

To distract his mate the next day, Keres led her down the hall after breakfast. "Let's go see your special room."

"You called it a nursery, Keres. Isn't that for babies?"

"Not only infants need a special nurturing place of their own. Look, here it is. Across from our chambers."

He opened the door and ushered Rimi inside. Stepping in behind her, he waited to see her reaction. "We can change anything in here that you wish."

"It's beautiful, Keres." She glanced around the room before walking toward the fluffy clouds painted on the walls. Rimi pressed a finger against the decoration. "It's like I'm in the clouds."

"That's what I hoped. If you would like, we can fly over Wyvern together and I can show you your new home this afternoon. It's raining right now, but it will be beautiful later."

"I'd love that," she said, before asking, "Is it safe?"

"For you? No outside dragon will invade our territory in Wyvern. If they do, that will be the last mistake they make."

"Really? No one will bother me here? I can fly around?"

"Yes, Snowflake."

She darted forward to throw herself against Keres' chest. He hugged her close and pressed a kiss to her uplifted lips. Instant heat flared between them. Keres deepened the exchange before forcing himself to lift his head.

"You, Mate, are a temptation. Before I tuck you in that bed for something other than a nap, go explore your room. You have to be eager to check everything out."

Rimi nodded and hugged him tight once again before stepping back. Under his watchful eye, she flitted around the room, trying out the big pillows on the floor and looking at the games in the toy chest. She oohed and aahed over the books on the shelves and moved them around to put the ones she wanted to read first on the right. He noticed her hand hovered over a book of dragon fairy tales several times, but didn't select it.

Keres reached around her and tugged the thick volume from its space. He glanced through it, enjoying the pictures. Rimi leaned against his side, seemingly interested as well. "I'd like to read this. Would you like to hear a story?"

When she nodded eagerly, Keres wrapped his arm around her waist and guided her to the large, oversized rocker. "Hold this for me, Snowflake," he requested, handing her the book before sitting down. He guided her onto his lap before reclaiming the beautiful hardback.

"What shall we read?" he asked and turned to the index. "Do you want to read about a gold or silver dragon?"

"Is there a black one or... maybe a crystal?"

"There is a crystal dragon here. Let's read that one first," Keres suggested and turned the pages.

"Check out this beautiful crystal dragon. He is very handsome, but your dragon makes him pale in comparison," Keres told her.

"You're a bit biased," she suggested.

Keres

"Of course. No one could out-sparkle my mate," Keres said proudly. "Let's see what happens."

Reading aloud, he started the story. It didn't take long for Rimi to relax against his chest. The story captivated them from the beginning. The crystal dragon was daring and brave. He detected the bad guys with his cunning skill and won the heart of a beautiful amethyst dragon.

Keres finished the story and checked in with his precious mate, "Did you like the story, Rimi?"

"It was amazing. Can we..." Rimi's question was interrupted by an enormous yawn. "Can we read another one?"

"Yes. The next one is about a bronze dragon. Shall we read that?"

"Bronze like Oldrik." She sighed and nodded.

Rimi closed her eyes as he read. Within a few minutes, her head dropped heavily to his shoulder and a slight snore wheezed from her parted lips. Keres rocked his mate gently and closed the book before setting it on the table nearby. They would read that story another day.

Holding his mate in his arms felt like heaven. Keres absorbed the sensation, fighting to keep himself from imagining what would have happened to them if he hadn't found Rimi. The madness that had threatened him would have overtaken his mind. And her luck in evading capture by another couldn't last forever.

But he had found her, and she had fought off the others. Keres pushed other possibilities from his mind. He brushed a lock of hair from her forehead. "I love you, Snowflake," he whispered.

"Daddy." She sighed and cuddled closer.

"Can we go fly?"

"Of course," Keres told his mate. "You lead us outside."

In moments, he launched himself into the air and looked back to see Rimi follow him. She was the most magical of creatures. His staff was completely used to seeing dragons shift, land, and take off. They didn't pause in their regular duties as he came and left. Rimi didn't notice the crowd that grew outside when she shifted, but everyone who could gathered to see the sun reflect on her breathtaking scales.

No one found her more beautiful than Keres. He flew proudly by her side as Wyverns gathered below, pointing into the sky.

There's a lot of people in Wyvern, she commented.

Yes, Mate. The horde helped gather all Wyverns back into the city after the change. Now the borders are closed so those inside can sustain their existence.

Is that a dragon down there? She pointed a talon at the center square of Wyvern.

It is. That is where all the mates are celebrated.

Celebrated? How?

Let's land and I'll show you. There is a space for dragons to land on the east side of the square. Keres led the way. He moved his bulk to the side of the wide area so Rimi could settle next to him.

A man knelt on one step. He'd turned around to watch them, holding tools in his hands. Keres and his mate had arrived at the perfect time. The worker smiled at the beautiful crystal dragon, obviously in awe of her sparkling appearance. Keres nodded at the stonemason. Thank goodness the skill of chiseling into the stone still existed. The workman inclined his head to both dragons and returned to his task, placing two more careful strikes of the mallet.

They are updating names on the steps.

Those are all the mates from the beginning of Wyvern?
They are. You can see Aurora, Ciel, Lalani, Skye, and Brooks there now.

The man blew on the riser before him, scattering small pieces of stone in all directions. After a quick brush with a large brush, he gathered his tools and moved out of the way.

Even in dragon form, Rimi gasped. She quickly shifted and ran forward. "You were adding me."

Keres mirrored her actions to stay by her side.

"Yes. I am twice blessed today. Once to record you as a mate and then to see you in dragon form," the workman said, bowing to Rimi. "My family has recorded mates since the pact began. It is an honor to meet you and to see you again, Keres."

"Thank you, Samuel. I'm giving Rimi a tour of town, and she spotted the dragon. Did your family also carve it?" Keres asked.

"Yes. My many times over great-uncle carved it from a huge chunk of stone. My skills are not so artistic," Samuel said, modestly.

"I'd be so afraid to make a mistake. You could ruin the entire stairway," Rimi pointed out.

"I prefer not to think about that, Miss."

"I bet," Keres said with a smile. "Thank you again."

"I have a great story to tell my kids tonight. They will be very jealous that I got to see the new crystal dragon," Samuel said before nodding his goodbye and walking down the steps.

Rimi dropped to her knees in front of her name and ran her fingers over the grooves. "I guess that makes this permanent."

"No, Mate. This makes it permanent." He lifted her hand to kiss the dragon pattern etched into her flesh. A thrill zinged through him at the light contact. Her eyes widened as she shivered in reaction.

Rimi nodded. "I'm glad."

"I am too, Snowflake. Shall we shift and continue our tour?"

"I'd like that, please."

"I'll show you where each of the dragons live. You can always find mine by the black stone. Oldrik, Ardon, and Skye rotate between their two mountains," he told her as he led her down the stairs.

"Are they close? Their territories?"

"Luckily, they're neighbors. Let's start there first."

Back in the air, Keres heard the faint sound of music playing. Could that be what Ardon had referred to yesterday? He tracked the sound and verified it came from the same direction.

Music again, he sent to the entire horde. *I am with Rimi. I won't leave the borders of Wyvern.*

Same direction? Drake asked.

Yes. I believe so.

Let's watch and see what happens, Khadar suggested.

Definitely. It could be a festival someone is putting on. Keres turned to look at his mate. Before her arrival, he would have flown that way to investigate due to boredom. She was his focus now.

Can we make another circle around Wyvern? Rimi asked him privately.

He nodded. Flying without fear was a new sensation for her. He didn't wish to cut her fun short.

Try this, Snowflake. Keres did a barrel roll through the air.

How?

Carefully, he coached her through some daredevil moves all young dragons learned. Her absolute joy went straight to his heart.

Wooohooooooo!

Chapter 12

Slate? Are you here? Rimi called her son.

I'm with Drake. He's teaching me to torch things.

Rimi looked at Keres. He didn't seem bothered at all that his son had asked someone else to teach him a skill. "Shouldn't you help Slate build his dragon skills?"

"I have and will. Learning from different sources is wise. Drake will show him something different than I will to create double the knowledge."

"Oh, that's normal?"

"Not at all. Most young dragons are either chased from the nest by their sires if they're still around or they're abandoned. Survival of the fittest at its best, I'm afraid."

"That's not nice."

"Slate will leave soon, Rimi. It will be tough for you to let him go, but his nature is telling him to find his destiny. Already, he's able to survive. After he gathers information from everyone, he'll be smart as well."

"I'm worried most about the threats I keep hearing about."

Keres nodded. "I am, too. It's too quiet. Something is brewing."

"Got anything else to distract me with before the hunt tomorrow?" Rimi asked.

"You've seen through my efforts, have you?" Keres smirked.

"It wasn't hard. So, what's on the schedule for today?"

"I thought you might like to see my hoard. We'll have to start one for you. Every dragon needs their own treasures."

"So, I get to take some of yours?" she asked, an unfamiliar greed bubbling inside her at the thought of precious collections.

"Calm down your inner dragon, Mate. We'll negotiate a few exchanges," Keres assured her with a glint in his eye.

"Exchanges, huh? What if I don't have something to swap with you?" she asked.

"Oh, I think you will. Interested?"

"You couldn't keep me away."

Keres reached into his pocket and pulled out a strip of black satin. "I'm afraid you'll have to wear this."

"You don't trust me?"

"Of course. This makes it more fun."

A thrill went through her. She couldn't mistake the sexual heat that had kindled in his gaze. When Keres twirled a finger to direct Rimi, she nodded and turned around. The satin felt cool and soft against her skin. It also felt naughty.

Keres wrapped an arm around her waist and guided her down the hall. Unused to not being able to see, Rimi felt instantly Little as she depended on him to guide her. Tracking the turns and twists as they walked through the mansion, Rimi was pretty sure she knew where they were. When a delicious aroma of Italian food wafted past her, Rimi stumbled. If they were near the kitchen, she was completely turned around.

"Maybe it's best if I carry you, Snowflake," Keres said and scooped her up in his arms with ease.

He walked so swiftly and pivoted several times. Completely disoriented, Rimi gave up trying to figure out where they were. She relaxed against Keres's powerful chest, trusting him completely. He rewarded her with a kiss on her hair.

"Almost there, Mate. Just let me open the secret passage."

Rimi tilted her head up. Maybe she could peek under the edge of the blindfold. Shoot. Nothing.

"Are you being naughty, Little Mate?"

She shook her head immediately. Rimi knew the consequence for naughtiness. "I thought I heard something," she made up quickly.

A gust of cool air drew her attention. She turned to scent the air. It smelled like earth and slightly stale. He jostled her slightly in his arms and she heard the sizzle of what she guessed was a torch igniting from the flash of heat and the burning smell. As Keres advanced, she listened closely for any clues. She could only hear Keres's footsteps and their breathing along with flickering and spitting of torches along the way.

Just as she'd decided they must be in a cave free of water and animals, Keres set her feet on the ground. When she was steady, he untied the blindfold, letting it fall away. "There you go, Rimi. Welcome to my hoard."

Rimi's mouth fell open as she scanned the area. The large cavern they stood in wasn't a man-made cave but a chamber she bet he'd carved out of stone himself from the gouges in the walls. She dismissed those facts as her gaze landed on an immense pile of gold coins.

They drew her forward until she stood at the edge of the collection. Some shiny, some tarnished, the coins appeared to be from many different countries and time periods. The gathering reached above her head and extended in all directions.

"How much is all this money worth?" she asked, mesmerized.

"A lot," Keres admitted. "Depending on the gold market, I

could buy a small country or a large one. Of course, everything can be bargained for now."

"I've never seen so many coins." Rimi poked her toe into the inches-deep puddle at her feet. She reached down to scoop up a handful. Spreading her fingers, she slowly let the money tumble to the ground. The metallic sound as they hit made her smile.

He thinks I'm naughty. I'll show him naughty. Concealing the last few coins in her hands, Rimi turned to distract Keres.

"Daddy? Coins are boring. Do I see something over there that sparkles?" she asked as she pointed with one hand and slipped the stolen money into her pockets when he turned to look.

"Of course. I should have suspected the jewelry would interest my sparkling mate."

Keres took her hand and led Rimi away from the overwhelming pile. He stopped just past the edge as he examined the wall. Following his glance, Rimi spotted white numbers glinting from a nearby ledge.

"Hmmm. It appears a few coins have evaporated," Keres noted.

"Evaporated?" Rimi asked as she furiously tried to figure out how to get rid of the coins in her pocket without him seeing.

"Metal doesn't do that normally on its own. Do you have any idea what happened?"

She shook her head automatically and stopped herself from putting her hand in her pocket. That would be a dead giveaway. "There's a scale under the pile?"

"Yes."

"I bet I kicked a few off the weighing area when I walked over there," she suggested.

"I don't think that's what happened." Keres ran his hands down her sides and stopped when he found bulges in her

Keres

pockets. "I think I have a magician for a mate." He unfastened her jeans and unzipped the fly.

"Wait!" Rimi said. "Maybe a few filled my pockets when I dropped them."

"Just jumped into your jeans?"

"The pockets stick out a bit. It might happen."

Keres lifted one eyebrow as he stared at her. Rimi held her breath as he considered that for a few long seconds. "Those coins could be sneaky. I guess I'll have to check everywhere now."

His hands slid into her open jeans and cupped her bottom, drawing her flush against him. She squirmed, trying to get away, and felt his thick cock respond to her movements. Snapping her head up, she met his gaze once again. Sexual desire shone from his eyes instantly, sparking her arousal as well.

Inhaling Keres's masculine scent, Rimi savored her mate's attractiveness. Everything about Keres drew her in. She leaned forward to press her lips against his. Immediately, Keres took control, cupping the back of her head to hold her steady as he explored her mouth.

Rimi threaded her fingers through Keres's hair and tugged. When he lifted his head, she whispered, "I think I dropped some down my shirt, too."

"I'm an excellent treasure hunter," he assured her.

Taking a reluctant step away, Keres knelt on one knee before her to strip off her shoes and jeans. He stood to turn her pockets inside out, clicking his tongue reprovingly when coins tumbled to the ground. "So naughty."

He tossed away the denim and stepped closer. "Let's see what else I can find." Keres tugged her T-shirt over her head and paused for a long second as he scanned her now nude curves. "Damn, I'm a lucky dragon."

Stalking forward, he cupped her breasts and lifted them to

his mouth. After pressing kisses across the full globes, Keres brushed his beard across her sensitive peaks, making her shiver at the tingly pleasure and prickle. He soothed one nipple with his tongue before pulling it deep into his mouth. Rimi tightened her hands on his powerful shoulders as he lashed his tongue over the taut bud.

"Please," she moaned and gasped when he bit his captive lightly. That taste of pain made her want more. "Daddy!"

Keres lifted his head to wink. He shifted his attention to her other breast. Rimi arched her back to give him full access. He rewarded her with caresses and passionate kisses. When her knees wobbled, his arm tightened around her waist, supporting her effortlessly.

Releasing her nipple with a pop, Keres pressed a kiss between her breasts. "Damn, Snowflake. You do things to me."

He scooped her up in his arms and carried her back to that vast pile of coins. Setting her gently onto the assembled money, he demanded, "Spread your legs, Rimi. Show me your sweet pussy."

Self-consciously, she widened her thighs. Would she look the same after pushing out the egg? She held her breath as he dropped to his knees between her legs. When his nostrils flared, Rimi knew he breathed in her scent. His eyes flashed purple with desire, reassuring her he wanted her.

"Snowflake," he growled and leaned forward to press a kiss to her mound. "I need a taste."

Rimi reached out for something to hold onto as he slid his hands under her full bottom and lifted her from the coins below her. Her fingers closed on handfuls of gold as her weight settled on his palms and her shoulders. She looped her legs over his broad shoulders and watched as he lowered his mouth to her pink folds.

Nibbling and licking, Keres tempted and teased her. Rimi

bit her lower lips, trying to resist the sensations building inside her. When he circled her clit with his lips and sucked, she lost the battle. Rimi screamed her pleasure into the vast cavern, and her voice echoed as Keres extended her climax with sweet caresses.

When he lifted his head, her juices coated his lips and beard. She dropped the coins trapped in her hands to reach out for him. Keres gently set her down to the pile below her hips. He leaned over her naked body to kiss her hard, demanding a response she was eager to provide.

When he moved away, a wordless sound of protest escaped from her lips. He roughly opened his jeans and pushed them down his thighs. She couldn't tear her gaze away as Keres wrapped his hand around his shaft, stroking himself from root to tip.

"Mmm." Rimi hummed her excitement and without thinking, licked her lips as she imagined his taste.

Immediately, he moved over her, his eyes dark with desire. Keres fit himself to her drenched opening and thrust forward, filling her completely. Rimi wrapped her legs around his waist, holding on as he moved.

Keres experimented with angles of strokes until she groaned with excitement. "There," she breathed. "More!"

Her mate increased his pace, pushing her arousal higher. The coins below her warmed from the heat of her skin, fueling her movements as she eagerly met his thrusts. She caressed his chest, tracing his muscles with her fingertips. His chiseled muscles provided her with eye candy that enhanced the sensations he coaxed from her.

Unable to resist, Rimi pushed her hips up to meet his next stroke. Her channel spasmed around him, drawing a groan from his lips. His jaw tightened, and she suspected he struggled for control. Rimi loved knowing she had that power over him.

"Temptress! You feel incredible," he growled as he slowed to allow her to recover.

When she curled upward to press a kiss to his lips, she whispered, "You do as well. Let yourself come, Keres. I love you."

He kissed her hard. Rimi clung to him, savoring his response. Keres would always have that fine line of danger. Getting that close to losing total control left a mark. He would never hurt her but would demand everything from her.

He snaked an arm under her hips and lifted her to meet his surge forward, reaching deeper than ever before. Keres staked his control over her. He powered in and out of her heat, tantalizing her.

Savoring the tingles that heralded her climax, Rimi tightened her fingers on his ribcage. She struggled to control her orgasm so they could come together. Losing the battle, she lifted her head and bit his shoulder as she shattered around him.

His shout followed hers through the vast cavern. The sounds blended together as they filled the space. She felt him fill her with warmth as he relinquished control. Rimi hugged herself to her mate, enjoying the intimacy of being one with him.

She could never have anticipated the joy that filled her life now with Keres. Rimi promised herself to savor the experiences he brought to her every day. She would never forget how he saved her along with himself.

"I love you, Snowflake."

"I love you, Daddy."

Chapter 13

Keres helped his mate up, loving how she trembled with the aftereffects from their lovemaking. He tenderly swiped a few daring coins that tried to cling to her skin and loved the imprint of others. Making love on a bed of money came with a few drawbacks but rated at the top of his dragon's heart. He took care to check her clenched fists and remove the coins she held.

"So naughty," he whispered before softening his words with kisses to her hands.

"Good thing you frisked me so thoroughly."

He raised his head to check her expression. Was she teasing him or upset? Her slow wink assured him she had enjoyed herself completely. He stepped forward to cup her bottom.

"I missed checking one place." His fingers trailed down the line between her cheeks suggestively. Keres loved the flash of red that colored her cheeks as she blushed.

"Not happening."

"Oh, it will happen, Snowflake, and even better, you'll enjoy it," he assured her, squeezing her bottom. He loved knowing she would think about that for a while as she bit her bottom lip.

"Come on. Let me show you around." He stepped back to take her hand, stopping her when she reached for her clothes. "I'm keeping you honest. No clothes for you."

She opened her mouth to protest and snapped it closed when he shook his head. "Fine. You have to be naked in my hoard then, too. When I have one, of course."

"Deal," he readily agreed and tugged her forward. "Let's go explore." He glanced at her as they walked forward and considered her love-rumpled hair. She was gorgeous.

"Are those tiaras?" she asked, pointing to a display in front of them.

"Yes. Let's choose one or two for you," he suggested.

"Really?" she squeaked.

"Of course. All dragons need jewels. Are there any here that you like?"

Immediately, she pointed to the one he would have chosen for her. A diamond-encrusted platinum frame glittered on the top shelf. It was perfect for the crystal dragon—almost as gorgeous as her dragon was. Keres lifted it down from the shelf for her and placed it on her hair.

"There's a mirror there," he directed, pointing to the right.

She walked like a child learning to balance books on her head—her hands out to the side. *Enchanting.* He moved with her to see her reaction as she reached the mirror. Her sweet lips rounded in an O as she took in the gorgeous tiara above the face of a well-loved woman. She lifted a hand to smooth her rumpled hair.

"Don't," he whispered, and she dropped it back to her side.

She met his gaze in the mirror and Keres told her, "Don't change a hair on your head, Snowflake. See how beautiful you are."

Rimi stared at herself for a few seconds before turning to

glide toward him. Her new confidence made him smile. "That tiara was made for you."

"Really?" she squeaked.

"That is a crown I collected from a princess in a snowy kingdom. I've had it for many years. None of my mates gave it a second glance. It has been waiting for you—the crystal dragon. The princess I've waited for all my life."

Tears gathered in her beautiful green eyes. Keres wiped those that tumbled onto her cheeks away with his thumbs. "Snowflake, what's wrong?"

"You've loved so many. I can't be special."

"I've had six mates before you. I have loved each of them completely and mourned their passings. Then you appeared, shattering my idea of who could be my match. You restored me. Do you know what excites me the most?"

"Slate?"

"I definitely wasn't expecting to meet my son if I'd ever had one. I thank you for him, but Slate will leave soon to lead his own life."

"Then what are you talking about?" she asked in confusion.

"You are a dragon shifter, Snowflake. You won't leave me. I get to keep you. I get to cherish and love you for the rest of my life."

She stared at him in wonder. "You'll want me for all that time?"

"Just try to get away, my precious Little dragon. I will spank off every crystal-colored scale on your naughty bottom," he threatened, giving her a fierce look.

It didn't scare her at all. Rimi reached up to smooth his furrowed brow. He could see her struggling to figure out what to say to him. *I love you, Rimi. Tell me you'll let me protect you until our last breath.*

Rimi met his gaze and nodded. *Until our last breath,* she vowed before saying aloud, "I love you, Keres."

Stepping forward, Keres wrapped his arms around her and hugged Rimi so close she squeaked. Then he spun in a circle that made her clutch at her tiara in panic.

"Keres! You'll make me drop my crown!"

Relenting, he slowed and set her feet back on the floor. "Sorry, Snowflake. You do have to take it off at some point."

"Not for a long time," she decreed, straightening the beautiful tiara.

"Want to choose another?"

"No. This is the one," she said without hesitating.

"Then, jewelry next."

Rimi dripped with necklaces and bracelets and held a couple dozen sets of earrings in her hands after the next stop. She'd had so much fun picking out treasures, he'd had to bring her a carved wooden chest to store the extras she couldn't wear. Unaccustomed to smiling, Keres's cheeks ached from his enjoyment of watching her.

"I can carry that," she said, reaching for the gorgeous box he held.

"I'll give it back to you, Mate."

"Promise?" Rimi stared at him hard.

"I promise."

She smiled up at him, making Keres feel ten feet tall. "Thank you. What else do I need in my hoard?"

"Gold, of course."

"Do I get that pile?" she asked, waving a hand back where they'd been.

"No," Keres answered. The heap of coins had skyrocketed in value to him after their play there. He wouldn't part with those. "I had something else in mind."

Waving a hand toward another section of his collection, Keres said, "Go through that doorway."

She winked and raced for the opening. Weighed down by the number of gems she still wore and holding the tiara, Rimi wasn't fast. Keres gave her a head start before jogging after her. "Wow!" reached him as he stepped inside.

That cavern was huge. In it, a fairytale castle stood. Rimi stood on the footbridge over the sparkling moat. "There are huge goldfish swimming around."

"Yes. Japanese koi. A couple of those are fifty years old."

"Does someone live here?"

"No. This is a play castle. If we dig through those stones," Keres pointed to the far wall, "it will connect to the east hallway. We can make a concealed entrance there into your secret hoard."

"This can be my treasure spot?" she asked, looking at the gorgeous castle.

"Yes. If you like it here. Let's go inside and you can see if you'd like to store your booty here." Keres stepped around her and raised the creaking front gate by pulling a looped chain. "Your kingdom awaits."

Rimi sped past him. "This is so neat."

He entered the large center room and leaned against the wall, safely out of the way to watch her cute bottom disappear as she darted into each of the rooms. Her exclamations warmed his heart as she discovered the play kitchen, the toy room, and finally, the bedroom with a wall of mirrors and a huge makeup mirror.

"Daddy! Bring my jewelry in here," she called.

Pushing away from the wall, he followed her voice. She knelt on the velvet stool in front of the large, gold-framed mirror. Gilded brushes and combs sat in front of her, as well as a padded head to hold her tiara.

"I love this room," she gushed.

"I'm glad. Where would you like me to set your collection? It will fit in this niche perfectly."

Rimi clapped her hands as he set it on the spot he'd created when he'd designed the castle. After his last mate had passed, Keres had worked on the castle as he dreamed of the future. When he failed to find a mate over and over, he'd spent more time in this area, determined to create something special for his fated match whenever he found them. Its vast size attested to the length of time he'd worked to create this.

In the last decade, he'd only visited to feed the fish and maintain the castle. Glancing at the sheer fabric draped over the small napping bed, he noted the bedding and curtains would need to be washed to rid them of the dust that had gathered. He'd wiped down all the horizontal hard surfaces the week before he'd left to search for Rimi. A quick visit while she slept last night had allowed him to be prepared for her first visit.

"Is this really for me?" Her smile faded slightly, and he guessed the cause of her waning excitement.

No one has ever played here before, Rimi. I created this for you. I filled it with love for my upcoming mate.

"Really? It's all mine?"

"It's yours. I'll help you connect to my mansion and we'll close the passage to my hoard."

"Will you have access to my castle?" she asked suspiciously.

"You are my mate. I will always have emergency use of any barrier between us."

Her face revealed her internal debate as she considered whether she wanted him to have the power to enter her hoard. "Will you take my stuff?"

"No. That would break the dragon code."

"There's a dragon code? They really should create a handbook for new dragons. We'll have to tell Slate."

"Slate already has figured that out," Keres assured her.

"Did he try to steal your stuff?"

"No, Snowflake. He's too smart for that."

"Oh, good. So, we dig? Do you have shovels?" she asked, scanning the area.

"Dragons do not need shovels," Keres said, and raised his hand, flexing his fingers like claws when she seemed confused. "Ready to get dirty?"

"Let's do this!"

Chapter 14

"Thank you for doing my nails, Daddy," Rimi said, studying the pale pink color he'd applied. Digging through the stone had done a number on her talons. She'd loved his pampering when they had finished.

"My pleasure, Snowflake."

"You really didn't have to seal that section between our hoards," she suggested.

He'd carefully filled in the passage with the stones they'd displaced while connecting to the hallway. Then Keres had heated them to melt the metal veins running through the rocks together to lock them in place. She could dig a door again, but he'd hear it for sure.

A shimmer caught her eye, and she launched herself from his lap to scramble under his desk. Grabbing the gold coin from the floor, she danced around it, chanting, "Mine, mine, mine!"

When he only smiled at her and wasn't concerned about having dropped the treasure, she studied him carefully. This was the third coin she'd found this morning. "Are you hiding these for me to find?"

"Dragons never give away their treasure."

"You already gifted me a bunch of stuff! Remember the tiara, the gems, the castle?" she reminded him, tapping her foot. "Admit it. You're leaving these for me to find."

"A shrewd dragon never questions the source of wealth. She just enjoys it."

"She does, huh?" Rimi considered the coin in her hand for a second and then thrust it into her pocket. She needed to cultivate her greedy dragon side. *Might as well start now.*

"Is everyone still coming over today for the hunt?" she asked, changing the subject.

"Yes. Look, here's Slate," Keres said.

"Slate, I think you grow two feet every time I see you. You need to spend more time with your mother," Rimi fussed, walking over to hug her son.

"Mom. I'm not a baby anymore. This hunt is more ceremonial than anything else. I've eaten a ton of cows from the field already," Slate told her.

"I've been meaning to talk to you about that." Keres drew his eyebrows together in a gesture Rimi recognized as the precursor of a lecture.

"Oops, it will have to be later. I think Skye and her dragons are getting ready to land," Rimi said quickly.

"Oldrik and Ardon haven't announced their arrival yet, Rimi," Keres told her, turning to stare at her in confusion.

Permission to land.

Of course, Drake, Rimi answered, before shrugging. "Sorry. I guess I felt Aurora arriving instead of Skye."

Keres simply shook his head and ushered her toward the door to greet their guests. Slate fell in behind them. She could feel his eagerness to hunt together with the group of dragons.

Is there any way Slate could remain here as part of your horde? she asked Keres.

No, Snowflake. I'm sorry. He's not part of our pact. Slate would not find a mate here. He needs to find his own place.

I'm going to miss him.

We both will. We'll have to practice making more dragonets, Keres suggested.

Meeting his gaze, she didn't need to answer. The silent message that flew between the mated pair said everything.

"Ewww," Slate commented from behind them, making Rimi laugh.

"Sorry." She lied. Rimi wasn't repentant at all.

As they emerged into the fresh air, more calls sounded as dragons and their mates arrived. Each of Rimi's new friends carried a large velvet bag. Soon, they divided into two groups: the horde and the excited, fated partners. When the sun became too hot, Rimi linked her arms with Ciel and Brooks. "Come on. Let's go inside."

"Good idea," Aurora agreed as she shielded her eyes. Lalani wrapped an arm around her waist and guided her toward the door. The others followed as they chatted.

We will leave as well, Keres messaged Rimi.

She paused and turned to wave. *Be careful. Take care of Slate!*

After watching their mates shift and take off, the group continued inside. The women took turns taking their tiaras out of the protective bags and pinning them securely in place. Brooks produced a crown made of rubies and diamonds that everyone admired.

As the group streamed into the dining room, Rimi waved everyone into their chairs. "Thank you all for joining me and having some fancy fun." She stopped and touched her tiara to make sure it was still in place before continuing, "I'm a little nervous even though both Slate and Keres assure me I don't need to be."

"Are you worried about the hunt or this tea party?" Lalani asked with a gentle smile.

"Both?" Rimi answered.

"I'd be nervous, too, if I had a child going off with the big dragons for the first time," Brooks admitted.

"No need to be nervous about us. We'll only bite the scones," Ciel promised and gnashed her teeth.

Since Ciel was the least threatening creature in the room, Rimi had to laugh. The others joined in, and the tension eased a bit from Rimi's shoulders. At least this part was going to be fun. She turned and looked out the window where the dragons stood together.

Aurora pointed at the youngest dragon as all of them launched into the air. "Slate is almost as big as Keres! Dragons grow fast."

"They do. Having control of all their powers takes a while to understand. Flying without running into something while you flap your wings, targeting prey with your flame, or grabbing at something with your talons is challenging," Rimi said.

"That sounds more complicated than some of the old video games," Brooks pointed out.

"I was always bad at those," Ciel confessed. "I just ran straight into the bad guys and died. Shortest games ever."

Laughter filled the dining room as everyone found their chairs. Keres's staff brought in fancy teacups for everyone and filled them with fragrant tea.

"I thought we'd have an almost traditional British tea. I hope that's okay with everyone," Rimi said hesitantly.

"I enjoyed afternoon tea in Scotland once. It was amazing. I ate so much I rolled out of the restaurant," Brooks shared.

"I'm crossing my fingers that you'll enjoy this as much. You'll find some of the traditional goodies on the displays as well as items I had the cook make for us," Rimi said.

The staff brought in three layered serving displays and placed them on the table between the mates to share. Everyone leaned forward to admire the display.

"Who knows what we eat first?" Lalani asked. "Brooks?"

"You eat the savory items first. Those are the items on the bottom here. There are two of everything, so each person gets to try everything," Brooks said. "Unless Rimi suggests a different way?"

"Heavens, no. I've been living in a cave. I just read about tea in a book and someone mentioned a tea party..." Her voice dwindled away. Had this been a good idea?

"This is so fun. Everything's so pretty. I hate to eat anything," Aurora said.

"No way. I'm starting with this one." Brooks helped himself to what appeared to be a cucumber sandwich. He took a bite and chewed with a happy expression.

That broke the ice. Everyone dug into their treats. "Mmm" and "Yum" sounded around the table. A few mates practiced drinking their tea with their pinkies out, provoking giggles around the table. The room grew quiet as they ate.

Rimi checked out the sweets displayed at the top and slumped against her chair back. She couldn't eat another bite. A heavy thud against the window made Rimi spin to see what had struck it. A purple eye stared inside. She jumped to her feet and ran toward the dragon pressed to the glass. "Slate! What happened?"

Her son's eye rolled back inside his head, and he disappeared from view. Her heart rate skyrocketed with immediate panic. Peering out the window, she searched for her offspring. Rimi's tiara tumbled unheeded to the carpet in her panic. Slate had collapsed in a pile on the grass below. She turned and ran toward the door, explaining, "He's hurt!"

Everyone leapt to their feet inside the room, knocking a

couple of chairs over in their haste. They immediately followed Rimi.

Outside, she ran to Slate's side and dropped to her knees beside him. Running her hands over his scales, she couldn't find any injuries, just something gritty. Looking down at her palms, Rimi rubbed at the powdery grit. Suddenly, she felt dizzy. Her head drooped down onto her son's body as she fought for consciousness.

Skye! Get everyone back. There's something coating...

Chapter 15

A deluge of cool water splashed over her skin. Rimi blinked, trying to figure out what was happening. Where was she?

Rimi! Slate! It's poisoned powder. We're rinsing it off. Don't drink any!

Skye's mental message echoed in her mind, and Rimi pushed herself up on an elbow. Immediately, the liquid streamed between her and Slate's bodies. Realizing she needed to get away from him so they could rinse off Slate's scales, she heaved herself backward, away from the dragon.

Good job, Rimi! That helps. Hold your hands out.

She followed the young woman's instructions. In a few minutes, the fog inside her brain cleared slightly. Getting that off her skin was working.

Skye, have someone run for brooms. Scrubbing this off Slate might help him. Don't touch him with your hands. It must absorb through your skin.

Breathing it in is dangerous as well, Skye told her. *I remember Daddy telling me that before. If we keep the water on it, it won't be airborne.*

Slate's groan was magic to her ears. He struggled to his feet, allowing the gathered mates and staff to scrub the powder from his scales. His thoughts were a jumbled mess that Rimi struggled to decode. Finally, her son's words made sense.

Attack. Plume. Sky. Dragons plummeted.

As Skye translated for the others, Rimi waited impatiently. As soon as everyone turned to her for their next move, Rimi told them, "I need you all to tell me everything about this powder and the previous threats."

Gathering all the information took time, Rimi suspected they didn't have. Unfortunately, she didn't have a choice. As the mates fell silent, she debated what to do next. Slate was still wonky. He was also young and inexperienced—not that she had a lot of insight into the world. She'd hidden in caves to protect herself for her entire life.

"We're not staying behind." Lalani's statement interrupted her thoughts. "They're going to expect dragons to come. Some of us sneaking in on the ground could be effective."

Rimi stared at the woman. Immediately, the other mates nodded. They all agreed. If their dragons died, they would most likely pass as well. Their minds and hearts were too intermeshed.

"How many of us can you carry?" Brooks asked.

"I'm not sure. I've never flown with anyone on my back," Rimi admitted.

"How far away is this, Slate?" Aurora asked.

The young dragon shook his head. He didn't have a clue. *It's outside Wyvern. We flew toward the sun when we left.*

So east of the city. Skye figured it out. *Had the sun moved toward your shoulder by the time of the attack?*

Yeah! It had. I'd ducked behind Drake in the beginning of our flight, but when the attack happened, I was flying next to him, Slate reported. *I'm trying to remember what happened, but everything is foggy.*

"Take your time, Slate. Tell us whatever you can as you remember. Thanks to that information, we can guess they're at least an hour out. Maybe two," Ciel said.

"With everyone on my back, I won't be able to fly as fast," Rimi pointed out. She noticed Keres' housekeeper and all the staff gathered around. They stood by to see what they could do to help. Even as stressed as Rimi felt, their support gave her strength.

I'm not staying here, Slate vowed. *If you leave me, I'll follow. I only came back because I couldn't save them alone.*

Rimi stared at him for a moment before nodding. "You hang back behind me. The mates will need you to drag them out of there if something happens to me."

"You're too sparkly," Aurora told Rimi. "They'll see you coming a mile away."

Rimi glanced down at the muck around her feet. "I'll roll in the dirt. That will keep my scales from shining."

Shifting, Rimi moved away from the remnants of the powder they'd washed from Slate. The workers wet a large patch of ground, and Rimi rolled in the mud. It felt cold and clammy, making this effort seem fated for disaster. Without discussing it, the mates who were dressed in light colors followed her pattern, even coating their blond hair.

Slate burst into Rimi and Skye's brains, sounding excited. *That dirt makes me remember something. Keres had soared high to check for deer. He messaged he'd found something strange. A distant settlement in the center of areas where the ground appeared to be excavated.*

My money's on that settlement, Skye announced. *Good job, Slate. Let's go check it out.*

Brooks and Skye climbed onto Slate's back as the others climbed onto hers. Rimi glanced at her son's dragon, immensely proud of his bravery. He didn't shy away from danger.

Rising into the air, she smoothed out her flight as much as possible for the three mates who sat on her back. She scanned the ground ahead, straining to see any trace of Keres and the others. Nothing popped out to her inside Wyvern's borders. Rimi wanted to speed forward as fast as possible, but she saved as much strength as possible. She would need it.

Rimi flew for an hour before dropping to the ground. She glanced up at the big white clouds gathered overhead. Studying them, she hoped to see them darkening to rain or even better, a storm. Perhaps water falling from the sky could work for them to rinse away the powder. Unfortunately, they remained fluffy and completely harmless.

We go on foot from here. Skye, can you pull the mates close? Tell them as we move, they should try to contact their mate. Warn the dragons not to react. Skye acted immediately. The young woman gathered the other mates and whispered into their ears. Immediately, their expressions became focused.

Slate, we'll cover more ground on foot and be less likely to be spotted if we split up. Take Brooks and Skye. Go that direction and circle around.

Following her own advice, Rimi reached out to Keres. He didn't answer her as she trod over the ground as quickly and as quietly as possible. Ciel, Aurora, and Lalani didn't speak. They hugged her back, not moving. She strained her keen dragon eyesight, trying to spot something. Nothing. Nothing. Nothing.

Ten minutes later, she froze and then flattened herself to the ground. Aurora, Ciel, and Lalani slid to the ground when she motioned them down with a slight movement of her head. *Slate! Skye! I can see Drake collapsed on the ground. I can see him breathing, but he's not moving. There are men and supplies with him.* She mentally sent a location marker to them.

Slate responded with his own location. He was to her right and circling the target from the other side.

Keres

Be safe. Do not do anything heroic, Rimi sent him.

She was surprised to discover that an eye roll could be expressed mentally. Rimi shifted soundlessly. Leaning to the side, she pressed her mouth to Aurora's ear and whispered, "I see Drake. Do not move. He's unconscious before us but breathing. I do not see the others. I'm going to sneak closer to see if I can find out what's happening and check on Drake."

Rimi waited as Aurora shared the message with Ciel and then Ciel with Lalani in a risky relay. Every hint of sound was a chance to be discovered, even at this distance. She signaled for the women to scatter to the left and she shifted back to her dragon. Pulling the elements of nature around her, Rimi faded from their view. Rimi heard Ciel gasp before covering her mouth to muffle the slight sound. Aurora reached out a hand and pressed it against her scales. She mouthed, *Wow!*

Rimi would have a lot of questions to answer—later. For now, she needed to get close enough to come up with a plan. The women faded away, following her request, as Rimi crept closer. A dragon moving stealthily seemed unimaginable, but Rimi had mastered the art of sneaking away over her long life.

She stopped a safe distance from Drake. A scattering of powder dulled his gold scales. It littered the ground behind him in an arc, attesting to a heavy impact. That actually pleased Rimi. The more knocked off his scales signaled a better chance he would wake up.

Three men scrutinized Drake. The large axes in their hands revealed the reason for their presence. She sent a warning to Slate and Skye for the group to be vigilant.

"How long do you think it will be until they attack?" a rough male voice asked.

"It depends. That small dragon may not have gotten back. You doused him well. He's probably dead a mile away."

The first man laughed, making Rimi's blood boil. "With

luck. A dead dragon is a good dragon." She steeled herself to remain in place. Slate was fine.

"They might send out scouts when they're not home in a day or two. That is, if they can find them."

"Wait. I thought we wanted them to come here," a high, reedy male voice asked.

"That would be easiest for us. We can take them all out with one fell swoop. But if not, we'll kill these while they battle to escape the craziness in their minds."

Rimi hated whoever that voice belonged to. He had to be the one in charge. Whatever had poisoned him against dragons?

"Sir Evan, I don't understand why these dragons are still alive. A bit more powder will end them," a shaky voice pointed out.

"I will keep that in mind, Chemist. These dragons are now bait. We will draw in the others to eliminate this horde. Then we go raid their holdings. Imagine the amount of money the dragons have collected over the years."

The guy in charge's voice again. *He must be Evan*, Rimi decided.

"Money is not important! They're vile, vile creatures. We must smite them from existence on the earth. Only then will the world return to its previous form." The man called the chemist's voice rose in volume like an old-fashioned brimstone and hellfire preacher.

Rimi steeled herself from shaking her head. They might see the movement. The chemist sounded like a zealot. He was the one the horde had run into over and over. She now knew what they were against—a brilliant mind capable of creating a substance that could end such powerful creatures. Unfortunately, his mind was twisted against dragons.

"If you gave us the formula for the dust, we could smite more dragons," Evan suggested.

"Never. Only I am the justice bringer," the old man yelled, shaking his fist at the others. "You are only my army of vengeance."

"Right. We foot soldiers will hang out here together," Evan said. As he turned away, Rimi could see his face had turned red with what she guessed was anger.

She edged forward slightly to hear what Evan said to the other men. The chemist turned his head toward her and Rimi froze. Thank goodness for the clouds in the sky that kept her shadow from revealing her presence. He would see her move past landmarks so she couldn't move. She forced herself to focus on counting the number of men gathered, instead of panicking that he could see her.

There are five men plus the leader, whose name is Evan, and a withered old man they called the chemist, who created the dust. Something weird is up. He can almost see me. No one should be able to detect me when I'm cloaked. Rimi controlled the shakes that threatened from the close encounter with the man who emitted pure evil.

Get out of there, Mom! Slate urged.

Soon. I'm going to scout for the others. Then I'll return. I want to monitor what's happening here. Where are you now, Slate?

His voice exploded with excitement in her mind. *Suddenly, I found an area that seemed familiar. We landed here when Keres alerted us. There was a lot of talk. I wanted to go hit them and didn't listen.*

Rimi wanted to yell at him but knew that wouldn't help now. *Scan for clues and then keep searching. You'll remember more.*

I'll try. Sorry.

This was a lesson he wouldn't forget. She changed the subject to tell them what she saw. *A half dozen tubes are sticking out of the ground, with a few bags of something nearby. They're loading them now. All the men are wearing light brown protective suits—except for the chemist. He's wearing plain cotton pants and a shirt.*

Rimi exhaled a silent breath of relief when the man's piercing gaze moved past her. Her camouflage was good, but not totally undetectable. She wanted to run far away from the danger that radiated from him. Unlocking her muscles, she forced herself to retreat stealthily. She needed to search for the other dragons.

From here, I can only see Drake. He must have gotten the farthest past where they initially launched the dust. The other dragons have to be around.

Slowly backing away, Rimi then circled back to where she'd left Lalani, Aurora, and Ciel. Shifting quickly, she relayed what she'd discovered and what Slate had remembered.

"Drake's there? Can I go see him?" Aurora pleaded.

Rimi's heart went out to the young mate. She didn't want to consider that Keres might not have survived. Her frequent messages to Keres didn't receive answers. "Men are patrolling around Drake with weapons. You'll endanger him if they think someone has discovered them."

Aurora nodded sadly. "I was afraid of that. At least I know he's alive. So, what do we do?

"We need to find the others," Rimi suggested.

The three mates nodded. Aurora close her eyes to concentrate one more time. She was sending another message to Drake. When she opened her eyes and shook her head, Lalani wrapped an arm around her waist in a consoling hug.

"Let's go find the others," Aurora said.

Zigzagging in dragon form with Aurora, Lalani, and Ciel on her back, Rimi searched for the others. Her heart leapt at the sight of two large lumps standing out from the green grass and brown dirt. The mates slid to the ground, freeing Rimi to move closer. Forcing herself to approach carefully and halt at a distance, she confirmed her find. Again, three heavily armed men stood close by to each of their bodies.

Oldrik and Ardon are here, Skye! They're breathing. There are men guarding him. Rimi sent a location to Skye. A wave of relief and gratitude flowed over Rimi from her friend. Rimi continued searching. Keres had to be somewhere.

I found him! Slate messaged triumphantly a short while later. *Keres is alone. No guards are here.* He was obviously circling around the camp to attack them from the other side, while everyone else on the hunt followed Drake.

Is he okay?

He's breathing. His eyes are open. I'm not sure if that means he's coming out of it or completely overwhelmed, Slate relayed. His mental voice sounded shaky.

He's fighting, Rimi told him firmly. *Wait! This must tell us their plan. They split up. Drake, Oldrik, and Ardon flew forward, straight toward the main camp. I bet I'll find the others soon. Keres had a job. Look around, Slate. What was Keres up to?*

A big barrel is close to him. It's labeled AgI. The barrel broke open when it hit the ground, but there's still a lot inside.

Baffled, Rimi asked, *Does anyone know what AgI is?*

Skye reported after a second. *Brooks says Ag is the chemical abbreviation for silver. He can only guess I is another element. He can't remember what that is. I wish my phone worked. I'd have an answer for you in seconds.*

We'll figure it out. Slate, move so the wind is at your back and blows over you to approach Keres. Try blowing to get the powder off him. If that doesn't work, you'll have to narrow your flame to a small beam, so the bad guys don't see it, and burn that crap off his scales.

Roasting my father doesn't sound like a good thing to do, Slate replied.

He's resistant to flame. You can't hurt him.

That's totally cool. My mom can disappear and my dad is flame-proof. I can't wait to find out what my specialty is.

Focus, Slate. Blow, then scorch.

Small beam. I'm listening, Mom.

You've got this, Slate. Thank you for helping.

Always. Now, let me work.

She continued searching. A few minutes later, a large green form rose from the ground. As she approached, a silver dragon came into view close by. Once again, Rimi signaled the mates she carried to dismount, and she shifted to share the news. *I've found Khadar and Argenis. From here, I can tell they're in the same state. Alive but not functioning. Again, a small number of men are with them.* Lalani and Ciel nodded bravely as they fought back tears.

Skye's mind reached out to her. *Are the guards with the dragons dressed in protective clothes like those in the main camp?*

Rimi reported, *I'm staring at this group now. These guys aren't. I don't think the others were. Why?*

If they shoot off any more dust, they'll sacrifice those guys. The guards have to realize that, Skye suggested. *Brooks came up with that.*

Everyone keep thinking, Rimi said. Something tickled against her mind. *Keres?* He didn't answer. That had to be him. Was he rousing?

Slate? How's it going with Keres? Is he waking up?

Maybe? If I could use a larger fire beam, it would go faster.

Broaden it a bit, Slate, but stay in control. Don't light up the area with fire. We can't warn them we're fighting back.

Chapter 16

Rain!

Rimi rocked back as if struck as Keres's voice boomed inside her brain. Still in human form, she wrapped her arms around herself. He was back!

Daddy! Are you okay?

That had to be Keres, Skye chimed in.

Silence followed. Rimi shook her head when the mates with her pummeled her with questions. She tried to listen for Keres to answer. When no further messages came in, she asked, *Slate?*

Busy.

Seething with frustration at not knowing what was going on, Rimi gathered Aurora, Ciel, and Lalani whisper close. She quickly clued them in as she waited.

Slate, you have to tell me what's happening.

Smart move, Mate, to have our son roast me alive. Keres's grim humor made her want to cheer, but who knew if someone was listening. She controlled herself with sheer willpower. *Keres! I'm so glad you're okay!*

Okay is a big stretch. At least my mind is starting to work.

Come to me, Snowflake. Bring the others here. When he lapsed into silence, she updated her small group before shifting quickly. Rimi messaged Skye as Aurora, Lalani, and Ciel climbed up on her shoulders.

Rimi moved as quickly as she could. Several times, she had to drop to the ground. The mates moved quickly each time to hide behind her camouflaging. Thank goodness they were used to mounting and sliding down a dragon's scales.

Finally, they reached Keres and Slate. The smaller dragon still attacked the dust. He currently treated Keres's rear legs. Rimi was relieved to see he carefully stayed away from the dust scattered by the black dragon's impact.

The mates slid off her back, and Rimi darted forward. Keres growled, *Stop!* The black dragon heaved his bulk upward and staggered forward to drop to the ground where no dust had scattered. Slate shifted and continued to attack the powder as Rimi rushed to his side.

He shook his head, keeping his scales away when she tried to rub her snout against his. *It's not all gone, Snowflake. Can you be brave for me?*

Of course.

I need you to take the remains of the barrel and fly into the clouds. Scatter the substance through the clouds. Concentrate it heavily on the areas over the dragons.

Why?

Silver Iodide will make it rain. Planes used to seed it into clouds for farmers who needed rain.

Does it work immediately? Rimi asked.

It will likely take hours.

Likely? Does that mean it could take longer than that?

Keres nodded his head. *It might not even work.*

They said they'd wait for a response for a day or two, she reported.

You've been to the main camp?

Yes, I was able to sneak close enough to hear. There's an old man. They call him the chemist. I think he's the one who created the dust. He hates dragons. He wants them smote down, she shared.

Of course, he does. There are always dragon haters.

There's also a guy named Evan. His men are providing the muscle. He's only in this for all the dragons' treasure.

Keres low growl made her smile. He was recovering more all the time. She continued to distract him. *There's no love lost between Evan and the chemist. My guess is they'd get rid of him as fast as possible if they could get the formula for the powder. The chemist won't give it up.*

Then, he's our target, Keres declared.

Tell me what I need to do.

This is dangerous, Snowflake. Even disguised, they're going to see you. You need to stay high in the clouds and dodge when they shoot dust at you. You need a spotter to tell you how to avoid the plumes, but there's no one who can go with you. Slate's still to wonky. He'd be dosed again in a flash. And he'd distract you.

I won't take another mate. They're too important.

Agreed. They aren't trained to hold on for dear life, either. Damn it! I wish I could shake this off. I don't think I can even take off. Keres tried to haul himself to his feet and knocked Slate onto his back.

The gray dragon couldn't stop his flame in time, and a jet of brilliant red and yellow fire erupted into the sky. A distant shout told Rimi and Keres that the bad guys had spotted it.

You have to go now, Rimi. Concentrate on the clouds slightly upwind from the main camp. Grab the barrel and go!

Rimi galloped to the cracked container and scooped it up, placing one talon against the gaping opening. She paused for a quick second to enable her talent and cloaked her massive form. The barrel should disappear from view as well. Unfortunately, once the AgI scattered from it, the mixture would no longer be disguised. Throwing herself into the air, she divided her attention between the men scrambling below her and the clouds.

Before rising over the clouds, she marked the line where the dragons had dropped as they tried to give Keres time to enact their plan to destroy the supplies with rain. Starting with the section she judged would drift over her mate, Rimi lifted the talon away from the barrel to allow the mixture to fall into the clouds. If he could recover first, Keres would know what to do to help her.

She had moved on to seed sections over the others when a gray shape flew past her, moving erratically. *Slate! Get out of here.*

Her son didn't answer.

Vowing to ground him for years, Rimi forced herself to focus. A plume of colorful dust almost reached her. They were targeting wildly hoping to hit something.

Watch out, Slate!

Were the clouds darkening? Surely she was imagining it. Rimi kept making passes across the clouds until the barrel was empty. *Please let that work!*

Slate, I'm out. Let's get out of here.

Rwahr!

Slate's outraged roar sent cold chills down her back. She looked back to see the remains of a column of powder dropping back to the earth, close to her son. They'd hit him.

Slate spiraled downward, heading directly toward the main camp. She had to save him. Dropping the barrel, she saw it reappear once out of her hands.

"There are two. One must be invisible," a loud male voice screamed.

"Don't panic. Shoot a barrage of powder around the area. We'll hit it," another voice ordered. *Evan.*

Rimi swooped under Slate's tumbling dragon and groaned at the impact. He was heavier than she was. Flapping her wings desperately, Rimi fought to carry his body away from the camp and slow down his descent.

Rimi! What are you doing? Get out of there. Slate's too big. Keres's voice sounded panicked.

Ignoring him, Rimi begged Slate, *Wake up! You've got to help me!*

The young dragon's mind spiraled as if he were caught in a hurricane. Rimi was on her own. She couldn't fight gravity with his dead weight on her back. The ground loomed underneath her. Rolling out from under Slate, Rimi held her breath as her son tumbled unhurt to the grass.

Rimi breathed a sigh of relief as she whirled to face the approaching threat. The chemist stood a hundred feet from her, and Evan's men struggled to yank a tube free from the earth to target her. She froze, hoping her cloaking ability would save her.

A rumble of thunder made the chemist glance up before he refocused on her. "Dragon, I see you. Your talent doesn't hide you from me."

Was he lying? Rimi wasn't going to fall for a trick. She kept her gaze locked on the dangerous man ahead of her. A rain drop landed on her right wing.

The chemist lifted his chin and inhaled through his nose.

He could scent her?

"Ah, a female. Of course."

More drops tumbled from the sky, wetting the ground around him. Out of the corner of her eye, Rimi saw the men attempting to protect the bags of dust. The sprinkles multiplied until the water ran off her scales.

"You might as well drop your camouflage, dragon. I can detect you now," the chemist told her, stalking directly toward her.

Spooked, Rimi's heart beat even faster until she was sure everyone could hear it. Still, she stood locked in place. If she moved, he would see her blur out Slate's form collapsed behind her.

Keres's voice filled her mind. *Hold on, Rimi. The rain is working. The horde is rallying.*

Rimi stiffened her back, bolstered by her mate's words. Gaze locked on the threat, she stood still. The man stopped a mere foot before her. Could he hear her heart racing? The chemist reached out a hand toward her snout. Automatically, she blasted him with fire breath.

The flames bent around him. Not a hair on his head sizzled. Surprise snapped her mouth closed, extinguishing the flare of heat.

Have you figured it out yet, crystal dragon?

The evil contained in that voice whispering inside her head made Rimi cringe away. She dropped her shield, and the men gasped as she appeared.

What are you? Rimi asked.

Get out of there, Rimi! Keres ordered.

She shook off his demand. Leaving her son unprotected would never happen. A clump of mud dropped to land by her talons as lightning flashed through the sky. The true color of her scales revealed itself as the rain rinsed off the muck she'd disguised herself in.

You're beautiful, crystal dragon. Of course, I couldn't find a female when I needed one.

You're a dragon?

Was a dragon. A pitiful creature driven crazy without a mate. Vengeance made me stronger.

A dark shimmer appeared around him, vivid even in the gloom of the thunderstorm. Rimi took a step back when he reappeared in front of her. A twisted figure of a dragon. She swallowed hard as she recognized the agony that had created the monster in front of her. His beast oozed with open wounds and rope-like scars. Only a few cracked scales remained attached to his withered hide. Rimi had no idea what color they had been.

I'm so sor...

I do not need your sympathy. Thanks to experimentation on this form, I created the substance that will end dragons. Sacrificing the beast that destroyed my mind was painful, but so worthwhile. Now, I am the master of all who shunned me.

The monstrosity took a step toward her. Petrified, Rimi retreated two steps without thinking. She fought her fear to remain in place, hoping Slate would rally as the rain washed off his scales. Forcing words to form in her mind, she tried to buy time. *I didn't wound you. I don't believe anyone in this horde acted against you.*

All hordes are the same. They would have destroyed the black dragon here if he hadn't found you.

You've watched this horde?

Yes. I observe many dragon units. When the black dragon was shunned as I was, I took revenge for both of us.

Keres wouldn't ask for this. He would never hurt the others.

The mangled dragon shook his head, managing to look disappointed in her. *You are delusional. Ask the others. He's already acted against them—scared their mates and endangered others. In fact, he will join me in my quest when you are gone.*

That won't happen, Rimi contradicted him, never more sure of anything in her life.

He will when his love dies before his eyes. I will show you soon.

Keres, stay away! Rimi sent a frantic message to her mate before straightening her shoulders to present a powerful presence.

Turning her attention back, she said, *Perhaps a mate could save you still.*

Even you, an elusive female dragon, couldn't save me now. Now, we have delayed long enough. As much as I enjoy sharing my brilliance with you, it is time for you to die.

A thump landed beside her. Keres. She didn't glance at him. Rimi couldn't take her eyes off the twisted dragon before her. A slightly smaller dragon moved into position on her other side.

Slate! No! Flee!

That eye roll again registered in her mind, almost making her laugh with the ridiculousness of his answer. Her son's bravery bolstered hers.

Hooray! The whole family is here. I can use two foot soldiers instead of one.

"Chemist! The powder is dissolving into the ground!" Evan interrupted.

I do not need more powder to defeat you. It has already weakened you. The black will protect his mate, leaving himself vulnerable. The gray is too young to be consequential. Once the crystal is gone, neither will have someone to fight for.

Rimi tilted her head. She heard something behind the dark words that should have terrified her. Wings.

"Dragons!" a man bellowed.

"What do we do? The tubes are filled with water," another yelled.

A blast of fire seared a path through the middle of the camp, setting anything flammable ablaze. Men scattered in every direction. Evan ran to the hideous, twisted dragon.

"What will work in the rain?" he demanded.

Power!

"He said power, if you missed that." Skye's voice called from above them as Ardon swooped over.

"Fuck that," Evan cursed. He ran into the now torrential storm. Most of his men followed. The few who remained threw handfuls of the disintegrating powder at the dragons and quickly learned how flambeed jubilee cherries felt when the poison melted harmlessly into the earth.

Rimi didn't flinch at the sound of their screams. Those men had harmed her family and friends. She blocked their payback from her mind.

With that problem handled, the dragons landed in a ring around those facing off against each other. Their mates slid from their shoulders and fled backward as the dragons stalked forward.

The encircled dragon twisted as if it was being pulled apart by an internal struggle. Clear black eyes met Rimi's. The dragon had overpowered his human side. The tortured beast roared into the air. Tears gathered in Rimi's eyes, recognizing his request to be destroyed.

Tell us your dragon name. She did not wish for him to die as the chemist.

Atropos.

Keres and Slate moved in front of Rimi, forcing her back. She stayed focused on the dragon whose human side had tortured and abused him. She didn't want him to die without knowing someone recognized his innocence in all the wickedness and malevolence of the chemist.

The black light in the dragon's eyes blinked out. The chemist faced them, once again in control of the beast. *This is not how my story ends. I am the creature destined to end all dragons.*

Atropos, Rimi whispered and repeated the dragon's name

over and over. Voices joined her. The other mates also chanted his name, paying homage to what the noble creature had once been.

Keres opened his mouth to blast flames at the chemist. Drake followed, and the others joined in one by one. The evil figure in the center made one last attempt to ward off his fate, ripping open his chest to pull out a bloody bag of powder. Before he could use it, Slate set it ablaze with a narrow blast of fire. The colored smoke rose with the heated air from the combustion up into the sky where the pelting rain doused the chemicals.

When only ash remained of the threatening figure, Rimi fell silent, with the others following her lead. One by one the dragons pulled back their fiery breath in the reverse order they'd joined the execution—Slate first with Keres extinguishing his flame last.

The rain continued to fall, washing all traces of the creature and the evil substance into the earth. The horde stood there, quietly mourning the suffering of Atropos. When the sound of the raindrops increased in Rimi's mind to a tormenting level, she shifted back to human form and threw her arms around Keres and Slate.

"It's over?" she asked through her tears.

Yes, Snowflake. Let's go home.

She nodded and lifted her face to allow the rain to wash away her sorrow. "Please."

Chapter 17

Keres rubbed the pink bottom stretched over his lap. "Are you ready for the last ten, Snowflake?" He reminded himself to maintain his stern expression despite her adorableness. He definitely couldn't condone her leading the other mates on a dangerous rescue mission.

"I said I was sorry. I couldn't just run away," she reminded him, looking back at him with tears streaming down her cheeks.

"You put yourself and the others at risk, Mate."

"I'd do it again," she told him defiantly.

"I know. That's why you have ten more swats."

"That's not fair. I couldn't keep them from coming. They would have walked there to help their dragons," Rimi protested.

"Do you want to make it twenty?"

She stared at him hard for a few seconds before slumping back over his legs with a disgruntled, "no!" Keres quickly delivered the last smacks and lifted her to sit on his lap. He controlled his smile at her hiss of discomfort. Rimi could toughen her hide by thickening the skin over her vulnerable cheeks, but she didn't make the mistake of adding extra naughtiness on top of the daring rescue that had earned her a spanking in the first place.

"No more risking your life, Rimi."

"I think you knocked off all my scales, Daddy."

He kissed the top of her head and hugged her close before wiping the tear tracks off her cheeks. He didn't think it was possible to love anyone as much as he loved his dragon mate. The next eons would not be enough time for them to spend together. "Your scales are fine, Snowflake. Your butt will sparkle just as beautifully as the rest of your dragon."

She relaxed against his chest. Keres loved holding Rimi and knew after her years of hiding alone, she craved his touch. He rocked her slightly to comfort her. After a few long moments, she leaned back to meet his gaze with a sad expression.

"I can't believe Slate is gone," she whispered.

"Dragons don't stay with their parents long, Mate. He's off to find a horde. I bet he'll contact you from time to time."

She nodded, sniffing loudly before asking, "Do you think Evan will cause any more problems?"

"I doubt it. Even if he had some of the powder left, he can't make more. It will disintegrate with time."

"How did the chemist get so many to work for him to attack us?"

"Some people need a cause to give their lives purpose. Those who view others with envy crave having someone to blame all their problems on. Dragons make a big target."

"That makes sense. It's so stupid though. Your horde has protected Wyvern for centuries and asked so little from the citizens," Rimi said.

"Our horde, Snowflake."

"I don't know how you've had multiple mates and survived. I dreamed the other dragons' mates grew old and passed last night. I'm still sad thinking about it and everyone is young now."

"I wondered what that nightmare was about. You should have told me."

"There's nothing you can do to change it," she said with an audible pout to her voice.

"I can remind you it's best to live in the present. Worrying about the future will cause you to miss precious memories you can make now."

Several long seconds passed as she considered his words. Finally, Rimi nodded and admitted, "You're right. I need to cherish my time with my friends."

"Exactly. Now, what would you like to do today?"

"Do we have to stay here?" she asked.

"No, we can go anywhere you'd like."

"I'd like to start at the dragon statue on the square, please."

"Okay. Any reason why?"

"I want to see it and the names again."

"Then that's where we'll visit. Tonight, there is a celebration in town following the harvest. I'd like to make an appearance there."

"Will the others be there?" Rimi asked, looking hopeful.

"They will. There's a theme tonight."

"A theme? Like everyone wears pink?"

"Kind of like that. But it's Dragon Day," he said, sounding slightly embarrassed.

"I don't remember hearing of a Dragon Day celebration before in Wyvern. That's really an oversight. The city should have celebrated its dragon guardians from the beginning for protecting all the citizens," Rimi said.

"From the horde's perspective, it should be Mate's Day. They are the ones who sacrifice their ordinary lives."

"I don't think Lalani, Aurora, Ciel, or any of the others

would agree with that statement. They didn't sacrifice their lives. They have wild adventures instead of everyday drudgery. Who else gets to rule the sky, flying on the back of a dragon stud who can shift into the most handsome and able lover ever?"

"Just an *able* lover, hmm?" Keres leaned in to kiss her pink lips.

Pressing her hands against his chest, Rimi pushed him away. "Don't get any ideas. You're not going to distract me from going on an excursion!"

"We could combine the two. A trip to an isolated waterfall and then..." Keres let his voice trail away suggestively.

"I don't have a bathing suit," Rimi said, waggling her eyebrows suggestively.

"Skinny-dipping it is. Let's go."

"Could we take a picnic basket with us?"

"Marvelous idea, Snowflake! Let's get you dressed and I'll go talk to the cook. He'll be delighted to make you a picnic basket of goodies. I think you have him twisted around your little finger."

"I didn't do anything special. I try to be nice to everyone. They all do wonderful things for me."

"Of course you're sweet to everyone. Would you like to fly with me or on my back?"

"I'll ride."

"How about we strengthen your wings by flying there together and then I'll give you a ride home?" Keres suggested.

"If you insist," Rimi agreed with a sigh.

"Thank you, Snowflake. I'll go organize our trip. Why don't you go play in your room for a bit while the cook throws together some sandwiches?"

When she happily agreed, Keres lifted her off his lap onto her bare feet. He quickly restored her panties, smoothing the gorgeous green silk over her blushing bottom. "Daddy loves your new undies. They're very pretty."

"They are!" She celebrated and pulled her top up to show off the matching bra. After he'd admired the pieces, he dressed Rimi in her jeans and drew her shirt back into place.

He'd gotten her a few sets of lingerie. Finding matching pieces in the right size was difficult, but two owners of an intimate apparel shop in Wyvern had searched through all their boxes to put together this pair and four others. He had repaid the shop owners' kindness by locating silkworms and a mulberry tree for them. If anyone could figure out how to make more of the soft material, those two determined women would.

Keres walked Rimi to the doorway of her room where she rushed in to reassure her stuffie, Rumble, that she'd survived her spanking. When she caught him lounging against the doorway, listening, Rimi had changed her story, embellishing the pain she'd endured.

"Snowflake," he'd warned.

"But I'm okay, Rumble. You don't have to worry. Keres is a very nice dragon who loves me."

"Thank you for clearing that up, Mate." Keres waited until he was in the hallway before chuckling at her endearing brattiness.

Do not panic, Snowflake. A copper dragon is coming in from the east.

We need to get out of here. We can go back and do something inside Wyvern. Rimi's voice was tight with tension as she scoped out their surroundings, checking for an escape route or shelter.

Stay calm, Rimi. You trust me to protect you, right?

Of course, but let's not test it.

Keres hid his amusement at her lack of faith. He had five hundred years on the other dragon and several tons of power. *You don't have anything to worry about, Snowflake. I promise.*

She turned her bright green eyes to look at him before. *Okay, but I don't like this.*

Duly noted, Mate.

The copper dragon had approached as if drawn by Rimi's scent. Then, as he came within a mile of their flying path, the dragon veered suddenly away. Keres roared after him to add another warning to whatever had caused him to leave.

He left. Her dragon voice revealed her surprise. *That's never happened.*

Our mating bond must keep other males at bay.

Does that mean I don't have to worry any longer? Your horde hasn't pursued me, but I thought that was because they're already mated.

That was my assumption as well. Or that I was too fierce for them to risk challenging.

Rimi rolled her eyes dramatically. *If the mate bond is the reason, I don't have to worry anymore.* She did a few celebratory loops, making him snort fire in amusement.

There's the lake. It's time to relax.

By the time they landed at the location he'd chosen, Keres could tell Rimi needed a break. Those extra swoops had challenged her endurance. Her beautiful dragon form needed to build up more strength. He would make sure she got more opportunities to enjoy flying.

Do we swim in dragon form? she asked when they landed.

He considered the gentle lapping water. Keres hadn't seen any predators in the water, but he wouldn't risk his mate. "It might be chilly. Let's start out wearing our scales and then switch to skin."

Keres led the way into the water, with Rimi following eagerly. He loved how her beautiful scales shone with the reflection off the blue water. Her heart-felt sigh of enjoyment made him happy. She deserved all the fun experiences in this world to make up for her rough start in life.

A splash of water caught him directly in the face. Keres twisted to meet the sneak attack, and Rimi's other wing lobbed the cool liquid at him. *Oh, you're in trouble now, Snowflake!*

Keres lifted his massive foreleg and stomped it down on the surface of the water, sending a tidal wave over her head. When it cleared, Rimi blinked her beautiful green eyes at him and sniffed.

That was scary, Daddy. I could have drowned!

He rushed forward to reassure her. When he was two steps away, she flipped her tail over the surface of the lake, pummeling him with water. Her hoots of laughter met him as his head emerged from the deluge.

Gotcha!

He shook his head and lunged forward. *You are in so much trouble for playing your Daddy.*

You have to catch me first!

Keres paused for a moment to allow her to dart away and then gave chase. Fish darted away from them, and songbirds fled the area as they romped in the water. The wildlife might never be the same. He had no idea how even a drop of water remained in the lake by the time he caught her, capturing her long neck gently in his jaws to pin Rimi in place.

When she shifted into human form, he followed her. She bobbled under the water, having obviously not processed how deep the water was where their dragons had cavorted. Wrapping his arm around her waist, he pulled her back to a spot where they could stand safely.

"That was so much fun," she told him, panting as she tried to regain her breath.

"I enjoy seeing you laugh," Keres told her.

"Guess what else I like?"

"What?" he asked, smiling at her cuteness. What was she going to come up with next?

Rimi reached up and pulled his head toward hers. She pressed her lips against his and kissed him enthusiastically. He loved how her tongue darted into his mouth to deepen the exchange. Heat blossomed immediately between them.

Keres hooked his fingers under the hem of her T-shirt and ripped it off. For once, he regretted that their clothes reappeared with their human forms. Now he wasted precious time revealing her luscious curves.

In a few moments, the water lapped over their bare skin. Keres caressed his mate, celebrating her full curves and beauty. Rimi stroked her hands over his chest and daringly traced his muscles under the surface. Closing her fingers around his shaft, Rimi squeezed.

"You're playing with fire, Mate."

"I can live with that." She drew her fist upward and whispered, "Show me what you like, Daddy."

He wrapped his hand around hers and moved her grip up and down. Quickly, her caresses became too alluring. "Temptress," he growled and pulled her fingers away. Keres trapped her hands behind her back with one of his.

"Daddy's turn."

Holding her securely, he powered through the water to the shore. Carrying her to a thick patch of grass only slightly wet from their boisterous play, Keres lowered her gently. Stretching out beside her, he gripped her wrists tightly when she tried to free herself.

"Daddy's turn," he repeated sternly, holding her gaze until she submitted. "Good girl. That deserves a reward."

He leaned over her and captured her nipple between his lips. Rolling it firmly, Keres then lashed his tongue across the tip. He loved her wiggles of delight under him. Her body responded to his touch so eagerly. After treating her other peak to equally delicious treatment, Keres drew before releasing her breast with a pop.

"Please," tumbled from her lips as she raised her hips to rub against his hard thigh between them.

"I'll make it better," he promised. He stroked a hand down her rounded belly and cupped her mound. Squeezing it gently, he treasured her moan of arousal. Keres brushed his fingers down the cleft of her pussy before dipping into her wetness. He deliberately targeted those special spots he'd discovered were her most sensitive.

When she twisted underneath him, Keres rolled to his back and sat up with her cradled against him. He guided her thighs around his hips and lifted her to hover over his throbbing cock. Teasing her entrance with the head of his erection, Keres coated himself with her juices before lowering her slowly around him.

When her pelvis rested against his, Keres pressed a hard kiss to her lips before warning, "Hold on, Snowflake. This is going to be a wild ride."

She wrapped her arms around his neck and squeezed her inner muscles around his shaft. "Make me come, Daddy. I need you."

Keres didn't need any encouragement.

Chapter 18

They didn't make it to the Dragon Day festivities until late afternoon. Of course, they'd had to enjoy the picnic packed by Keres's cook. Rimi didn't want to be rude, of course.

She could tell by the expression on the other mates' faces as she floated the luncheon excuse by them that they questioned what actually had delayed Keres and her arrival. Quickly, she distracted them.

"I wanted to go see the dragon statue. Does anyone wish to come with me?"

"Argenis said all the names are there now. Let's go check it out." Ciel chimed in her support of that idea.

"Stay together," Drake warned.

"Of course," Aurora promised.

They walked two blocks from the festival site to the main town square. Everyone greeted them along the way, wishing them health and happiness. Several small children gave them flowers and blew kisses to them.

It was impossible not to be swept up in the day's excitement. Approaching the stairs leading up to the ancient dragon statue, the group stopped when they reached the base. Flowers lined each step in a gorgeous display of color.

The amount of time it must have taken the townsfolk to gather and place all those blossoms astounded Rimi. She clasped her hands to her heart as her gaze ran over all the names from the most ancient on top toward the bottom.

Aurora's name was first for their group, of course. It must have been scariest for her without any other new mates to talk to. Aurora had welcomed those who came after her with warmth. She'd answered questions openly and honestly to make the next mates' transitions as easy as possible.

Ciel, Lalani, Skye, and Brooks's names followed Aurora's. Each had connected with the others and, in turn, helped the next arrival acclimate. Rimi loved each of them. She'd never had friends, but knew deep inside these special, fated mates were more than simple acquaintances. They'd become family.

Rimi stared at her name. Next to the final letter of her name was an addition she hadn't seen before. With no last name like the others, Samuel, the stone mason, had returned to add a special character for her. A small dragon's footprint (or would that be claw mark?) decorated her name on the right. She loved it.

"Look, Rimi! You're the only one with a dragon print. Everyone will remember for eons how special you are!" Ciel said.

Linking her elbow with her friend's arm, Rimi corrected her firmly. "We're all special. Think how many Wyverns there have been since the founding families signed the pact. The odds of us being a fated mate are astronomical."

An older woman moved up beside them, carrying a heavy tome in her hands. Brooks smiled at his grandmother, Elenore, who'd emerged as the spokesperson for the current Guardians of their founding family's tome. "The city of

Wyvern can never celebrate you enough. Thank you for caring for our dragons. Without you all to tether them to sanity and our world, Wyvern would have been lost centuries ago."

"I think I can speak for the others," Lalani spoke quietly. "We only followed our hearts."

"That is the best reason to choose your path in life," Elenore assured them with a smile.

Rimi? Are you safe? Keres messaged her.

Yes, my love. We are. I'll return in a few moments.

Do not stay away too long. I miss you.

She smiled at the black dragon's message. Rimi doubted whether anyone could have foretold his destiny—from struggling to maintain his sanity to caring Daddy.

"Drake is getting impatient. I should go back," Aurora said.

"Ditto," Brooks echoed. "Let's all go together."

"I don't think you're going anywhere," a hauntingly familiar voice said from behind them.

Evan! Skye broadcast a message to Rimi and their dragon shifter mates.

Without a moment's hesitation, Elenore whirled and smacked the side of Evan's head squarely with the heavy tome she held. The evil henchman tumbled to the ground. The Wyverns who had gathered in the town square for the celebration quickly realized what was going on from the mates' reactions. After a quick scuffle, they secured the handful of men and women who'd stood at Evan's back.

Rimi looked at the crowd in amazement. "Thank you all. Elenore...." She had no idea what to say to the elderly woman.

"What the he... heck, Grandma." Brooks corrected himself as he spoke.

"Brooks made me promise not to let anything raise my blood pressure. Whacking that scoundrel with the book seemed to be an effective way to solve two problems simultaneously. Oh, dragon feathers. That jerk's hard head tore the binding."

"We'll find an expert to fix it, Grandma," Brooks assured her, taking the heavy volume from her hands.

"We'll need to. I trust the dragons will stick around for hundreds of more years. The future Battlefields will need to know their commitments," Elenore said proudly. "Speaking of dragon assistance, Brooks, could you sweet-talk Rogan into going to pick up your cousin Amber and her family? She would be perfect as the next Guardian for our family."

"Grandmother? What are you telling me? Is something wrong with you?"

"Heavens, no. At least nothing more than was wrong with me last week. Just planning ahead, Brooks." When Elenore noticed everyone eavesdropping on their conversation, she added, "Oh, my. I'm interrupting the celebration. We'll talk later."

"We will," Rogan assured her with a nod.

Their dragons had arrived with a flurry of commotion and worry, along with the volunteer authorities. The latter immediately secured Evan's crew and their still unconscious boss. Elenore and that book packed a wallop.

"Are you okay, Snowflake?" Keres asked, wrapping his arms around her after everything settled back to a joyous celebration.

Rimi nodded and hugged him hard. "I'm okay. Wyverns protected us."

"Of course they did. The pact was never designed to be a one-way street, but a symbiotic relationship where we take care of each other. That's how Wyvern has survived all these years."

Mom! Dad! I've found a horde that has an opening. Well, it's the second one I've found. The first one was definitely more predatory than I wanted.

Slate? Are you okay? Rimi could sense an underlying sense

of pain from her son even from the long distance away. Had that first horde hurt him? Her mom instincts jolted her into readiness to kick some dragon booty. Keres bristled beside Rimi. She patted his chest to calm her mate as the other dragons headed their way to find out what had put the black dragon on edge.

Wiser, but okay. I don't need you to go ninja on them. I'm going slower with this second group.

Smart, Slate. There aren't many new dragons born. Remember, they need you as much as you'd benefit from them.

Come home and visit? Rimi suggested.

Someday, Mom. Dad, take care of her, Slate requested with steel in his voice that made Keres smile.

Will do, Slate. Thanks for messaging us.

Slate? Rimi wanted to ask a million more questions, but her son had cut the connection.

Looks like we'll have to make another one, Snowflake. I'm up for practicing.

Rimi blushed, remembering how good their lovemaking was together. When the mates laughed at her expression, she knew they had no doubt something intimate was going through her mind. Already, they knew her too well.

"Come on, Rimi. Let's go get a slice of pizza. Angelino is cranking them out tonight," Brooks suggested, taking her hand to tug her away from Keres. The others swarmed around her and they whisked her into the crowd.

Rimi smiled over her shoulder at Keres, who laughed at the mates' antics. The other dragon shifters slapped him on the back, having fun as well. He was part of the horde. They hadn't given up on him and wouldn't now. Losing herself in the celebration, Rimi didn't pause to compare her previous existence to her life now. Keres had rescued her, and she saved him. The creators of the pact between the dragon and Wyverns couldn't have known the impact of their agreement. But the dragons would continue to protect the citizens from all forms of evil, no matter what happened in the future. Only the luckiest of the citizens would experience a fated mate bond.

Rimi spotted a lopsided dragon drawn on the back of a teenager's hand as she leaned against a nearby pillar. The young woman watched the dashing male dragon shifters celebrating with their mates. Could a dragon shifter's love await her in a few years?

Only if fate smiled upon her.

Thank you for reading Keres: Fated Dragon Daddies 6!

Don't miss future sweet and steamy Daddy stories by Pepper North? Subscribe to my newsletter!

I'm excited to offer you a glimpse into The Magic Of Twelve: Violet, an International Bestselling novel introducing a magical world where you'll meet the massive Sorcerers of Bairn and their cherished Little ones in this heat-meets-sweet romance series!

5.0 out of 5 stars
A very unique story concept!
This book was a lot of fun! Very unique from any romance and any age play books I've read before. It was a blend of both of those things AND sorcery/magic. Very unique.

This set up the series fantastically and I can't wait to see how things unfold. But what I'm really excited for is to see what happens after all 12 woman are with their sorcerer daddies.

I enjoyed Violet's rebellious/defiant streak. Those are always my favorite types of characters to read, those that are strong willed and strong minded. Gotta give that Pappa a run for his money! 😊

5.0 out of 5 stars
Papa!
Paranormal Daddy, yes please! This is the beginning of what promised to be a fantastic series. Magic, mayhem, and bigger than life Daddies to save the littles (droblins). I highly recommend!

Pepper North

The Magic Of Twelve: Violet
Chapter One

Violet DuMass dropped her purse on the entryway table and shrugged her coat from her shoulders. She was a little tipsy from the happy hour margarita that she had enjoyed with a group of colleagues after work to celebrate her twenty-second birthday. Turning, Violet double-checked that the deadbolt on the door was locked. Her shoulders sagged a little in relief. She'd had a strange feeling that someone had been watching her today. She kept looking over her shoulder and around the office building, but she never caught anyone looking at her strangely.

Breathing a sigh of relief, she walked down the hall unbuttoning the pale pink blouse her mother had sent her for her birthday. It was one of the only clothing presents she had ever received from her mother that she would actually wear. *Maybe her taste is improving.* Violet laughed at the thought. As she approached her bedroom door, she reached down and pulled off her high heels. Wiggling her toes in relief, she walked into her room and put the heels in her closet.

Something caught her eye. A strange fluttering motion seemed to ripple in the antique mirror that she had brought with her when she moved out of her parents' home. She'd always loved the gilt frame that encircled it. Heavens knows as a teenager she'd spent enough time peering into it, hoping to magically be transformed into a ravishing beauty.

As she walked forward to look closer, Violet saw her reflection. Still no ravishing beauty, but she considered herself nice to look at with long, deep brown hair and the eye-catching violet eyes that had inspired her name. Her lips were full and usually smiled with an enjoyment of life. She brushed her bangs out of her eyes and leaned closer.

There! There it was again. It looked like a butterfly was trying to flutter its way through the mirror. Violet reached a tentative hand up to the mirror and touched the cool surface. A dramatic flash of light burst around her, and Violet felt herself being pulled forcefully through the mirrored surface.

She tumbled forward and pressed her shaking hands against a sparkling white marble floor. Glancing up in confusion, Violet scrambled to her bare feet and looked around in shock. This was not her apartment. She clutched the front of her blouse together in her hands. She was in a large room decorated as if it was a receiving chamber in a medieval Italian palace. Turning, she saw the twin of her mirror hanging behind her on the wall. She raced back to it, slapping her hands frantically to the cold surface. It was solid. She ran her fingers along the sides of the heavy frame but found nothing. Violet turned shaking to press her back against the wall. She had taken a self-defense class last year, and she remembered the instructor stressing that this was the only way to be safe from at least one side. It was also a good way to get trapped, but she wasn't going to think about that possibility.

Looking around the area, Violet was bewildered. The room she was in had a mixture of old, new, and weird items all gathered together. In the corner was a desk with a laptop computer but over in front of the lighted panel was an old-fashioned spyglass. There was a cabinet on the opposite wall filled with antique apothecary jars and vials.

"Where am I?" Violet whispered to herself just to hear her own voice and know that she was awake. "What did they put in that margarita?"

A deep voice came from the arched doorway to her right. "I wondered when you would arrive. It is 7:23, one minute after your birth, twenty-two years ago." She twisted her neck quickly to look at him. He was massive, at least seven feet tall with a wide chest and shoulders. A black beard and mustache covered the lower third of his face. His shiny black hair was braided intricately down the back of his head, and the tail of the braid lay thick and heavy over his shoulder. Dangling from his left ear was a polished, intricate steel earring.

"Ummmm, I'm not sure where I am. There must have been some mistake. I know this is going to sound crazy, but I just touched the surface of my old mirror and . . ." Violet attempted to explain.

"And you fell through the mirror, landing here in my study," he completed easily. "Welcome to your new life," he said dryly. "I have been waiting for you to become an adult and come to me for many years, Violet. Now, let's get you settled in," the man began as he waved his hand in an intricate pattern through the air.

Violet felt her clothes begin to slide from her body. She attempted to hold on to each piece, but they slipped through her fingers. Finally, she stood in front of the strange man wearing only her white lace bra and panties. Wrapping her arms around her torso to shield herself from his view, Violet blustered, "I don't know how you did that, but you have no

Keres

right to take my clothing, sir. Give them back immediately. Who do you think you are?"

With a casual wave of his hand, her arms straightened and froze by her sides. "Your old clothes are no longer necessary for you. You're not in Atlanta anymore. Here, I decide what you wear or don't wear." He flicked his fingers, and her bra and underwear disappeared.

Using all her strength, Violet strained to cover herself, but she was held solidly in place. She opened her mouth to scream but found her lips sealed together. "Aarrrrggghhhh!" the muffled sound stilled in her throat. She watched in horror as the man approached her silently stopping several feet away. His ice-blue eyes ranging over her exposed body as he gestured once again, and her feet slid across the floor to stop in front of him.

"I am Garrick. You were matched with me twenty-two years ago. I'm assuming your earth government has not revealed its agreement to allow the collection of children who are the destined ones for the Sorcerers of Bairn?" He chuckled at the look in her eyes. He waved a finger releasing her mouth to speak.

"Are you mad? There isn't any Earth government. There are separate countries all over Earth that make their own rules and treaties. And really? The Sorcerers of Bairn? I can't think of anything that sounds more made up! Maybe the term destined ones!" indignant words burst from her mouth before once again with a finger movement her lips were sealed. "Aarrrrggghhhh!"

"Now, I can see why your destiny completes mine. Your form is beautiful, but your fire and spirit will keep me on my toes for a millennium. Since you have amused me, I will answer your questions. The leaders of each country on Earth were gathered at the great hall. Each decided to sign the agreement so that they would be returned to Earth safely. There are many destined ones here from a variety countries. You see, the Sorcerers of Bairn are blessed at birth to receive an abundance powers. We take a lifetime oath to practice and hone our magical abilities, but we do not achieve our full power until our destined one reaches maturity and appears in our homes. You are very lucky to be my mate. I already have extremely strong powers. You will make me even more powerful."

Garrick walked toward her. His size loomed over her as he approached. "I have been waiting for you since before your birth. I welcome you, Violet, to my home. I hope you will be happy here. You will never return to your old life. Already, your life there has been erased." With a click of his fingers, a window appeared to show the view of Violet's parents standing in mourning clothes next to a newly dug grave. The image ended as it narrowed in to show her mother blowing a kiss toward the casket as it was lowered into the ground. With another click of Garrick's fingers, the picture dissolved.

"It will be your choice to live looking back at your past, or to explore the possibilities that reach into the future." He extended a huge hand toward her, and Violet felt her arm straighten to raise her hand to lay upon his. "It is done," Garrick said ominously, and a lightning bolt of energy jolted down from out of nowhere to surge painfully through their joined hands.

Instantly tears of agony welled into Violet's eyes. Garrick waved his other hand through the air, and a cooling burst flowed across her burning skin. Holding their hands together, he looked deep into her eyes. "I am glad you are here, Violet. I will take good care of you. I promise." And he caught her gently as she fainted and crumpled to the ground.

Want to read more? One-click The Magic Of Twelve: Violet

Read more from Pepper North

Devil Daddies

The members of the Devil Daddies MC will risk all to secure two things: special acquisitions and women with a Little side.ly guard his mate from harm.

Fated Dragon Daddies

Change is coming to Wyvern.
A centuries-old pact between the founders and their powerful allies could save the inhabitants of the city once again, but only a dragon Daddy can truly guard his mate from harm.

Shadowridge Guardians

Combining the sizzling talents of bestselling authors Pepper North, Kate Oliver, and Becca Jameson, the Shadowridge Guardians are guaranteed to give you a thrill and leave you dreaming of your own throbbing motorcycle joyride.

Are you daring enough to ride with a club of rough, growly, commanding men? The protective Daddies of the Shadowridge Guardians Motorcycle Club will stop at nothing to ensure the safety and protection of everything that belongs to them: their Littles, their club, and their town. Throw in some sassy, naughty, mischievous women who won't hesitate to serve their fair share of attitude even in the face of looming danger, and this brand new MC Romance series is ready to ignite!

Danger Bluff

Welcome to Danger Bluff where a mysterious billionaire brings together a hand-selected team of men at an abandoned resort in New Zealand. They each owe him a marker. And they all have something in common–a dominant shared code to nurture and protect. They will repay their debts one by one, finding love along the way.

A Second Chance For Mr. Right

For some, there is a second chance at having Mr. Right. Coulda, Shoulda, Woulda explores a world of connections that can't exist... until they do. Forbidden love abounds when these Daddy Doms refuse to live with regret and claim the women who own their hearts.

Little Cakes

Welcome to Little Cakes, the bakery that plays Daddy matchmaker! Little Cakes is a sweet and satisfying series, but dare to taste only if you like delicious Daddies, luscious Littles, and guaranteed happily-ever-afters.

Pepper North

Dr. Richards' Littles®

A beloved age play series that features Littles who find their forever Daddies and Mommies. Dr. Richards guides and supports their efforts to keep their Littles happy and healthy.

Note: Zoey; Dr. Richards' Littles® 1 is available FREE on Pepper's website:
4PepperNorth.club

Dr. Richards' Littles®
is a registered trademark of
With A Wink Publishing, LLC.
All rights reserved.

SANCTUM

Pepper North introduces you to an age play community that is isolated from the surrounding world. Here Littles can be Little, and Daddies can care for their Littles and keep them protected from the outside world.

Soldier Daddies

What private mission are these elite soldiers undertaking? They're all searching for their perfect Little girl.

The Keepers

This series from Pepper North is a twist on contemporary age play romances. Here are the stories of humans cared for by specially selected Keepers of an alien race. These are science fiction novels that age play readers will love!

The Magic of Twelve

The Magic of Twelve features the stories of twelve women transported on their 22nd birthday to a new life as the droblin (cherished Little one) of a Sorcerer of Bairn. These magic wielders have waited a long time to take complete care of their droblin's needs. They will protect their precious one to their last drop of magic from a growing menace. Each novel is a complete story.

Keres

Ever just gone for it? That's what *USA Today* Bestselling Author Pepper North did in 2017 when she posted a book for sale on Amazon without telling anyone. Thanks to her amazing fans, the support of the writing community, Mr. North, and a killer schedule, she has now written more than 180 books! Enjoy contemporary, paranormal, dark, and erotic romances that are both sweet and steamy? Pepper will convert you into one of her loyal readers. What's coming in the future? A Daddypalooza!

Sign up for Pepper North's newsletter

Like Pepper North on Facebook

Join Pepper's Readers' Group for insider information and giveaways!

Pepper North

Follow Pepper everywhere!
Amazon Author Page
BookBub
FaceBook
GoodReads
Instagram
TikToc
Twitter
YouTube
Visit Pepper's website for a current checklist of books!

Printed in Dunstable, United Kingdom